The Badgers
of Summercombe

by Ewan Clarkson

SYLA, THE MINK
HALIC: THE STORY OF A GRAY SEAL
THE RUNNING OF THE DEER
IN THE SHADOW OF THE FALCON
WOLF COUNTRY: A WILDERNESS PILGRIMAGE
THE BADGERS OF SUMMERCOMBE

The Badgers
of Summercombe

EWAN CLARKSON

A Sunrise Book

E. P. DUTTON | NEW YORK

LIBRARY OF CONGRESS CATALOGING IN PUBLICATION DATA

Clarkson, Ewan.
  The badgers of Summercombe.

  "A Sunrise book."
  I. Title.
PZ4.C6123Bad3   [PR6053.L36]   823'.9'14   76-41219

ISBN: 0-87690-230-1

Published simultaneously in Canada by Clarke, Irwin & Company Limited, Toronto and Vancouver

10 9 8 7 6 5 4 3 2 1

First Edition

To June. For Andrew.

Contents

1. The Hollow Hill

It was raining again. Tobar lay just inside the entrance of the hole beneath the tree, listening to the drip of moisture from the leafless branches, sniffing the warm, damp wind that swept in from the Atlantic Ocean, and brought with it dense gray clouds that condensed into countless shimmering droplets, to silver the turf and stain the old yellow limestone rocks. Somewhere a blackbird sang a throaty serenade to this, the false promise of spring, for although the days were lengthening, and the sun, when it shone, held a soft warmth, winter could still return, locking the land in frost, and blanketing the fields with drifting snow.

Now, as daylight faded almost imperceptibly into the gathering gloom of dusk, the blackbird settled to roost in the elder thicket, and Tobar emerged into the open, his nose still questing the air and his ears alert for any hint of impending danger. Once satisfied that all was well, he set off at a brisk trot, down through the wood and into the valley.

Five hundred years before the birth of Christ, a band of savage and warlike people had come north out of the marshlands of Somerset, carrying weapons and implements of iron, and driving before them flocks of sheep, goats, and scrawny cattle. They were looking for land, well-drained, fertile land on which they could graze their herds, grow their meager crops, and where, if necessary, they could defend themselves against attack.

They came at last to this valley, hidden in a fold of the hills. Here the slopes were gentle and sun-warmed, sheltered from the cold winds that blew from the east and north, and the floor of the valley was wide and flat, a series of ancient meadows created by the labors of generations of beaver. Above the valley towered a hill, a weather-worn outcrop of limestone rock, and here on the plateau, close by a spring, they built their fort, a sturdy structure of timber and stone, surrounded by a wall and ditch.

Below, on the wooded slopes of the hill, where the rocks lay so close to the surface that their craggy heads were exposed, was another stronghold, a labyrinth of tunnels and passages dug deep into the hollow of the hillside. This fort was old before the coming of men, so old that its origins are lost in the unwritten annals of prehistoric time.

The Iron men are gone now, and their passing was so long ago that of their existence there is now barely a trace. Sheep graze where the fortifications once stood, and flowering grasses shiver in the breeze that blows eternally across the summit of the hill. Yet in the stronghold under the earth, life remains the same, for while down through the ages mankind has repeatedly changed his lifestyle, hoping each time that the new way would prove more successful than the last, the badgers of Summercombe have kept to the old ways, the ways that have served them well, that serve them still.

The European badgers are a proud and ancient race. There were badgers in Britain before the ice age, before primitive man crossed the marshy plains that are now the North Sea. A badger watched as the Bronze men hauled the mighty stones across the plains for the building of Stonehenge. A badger hid in a thicket as the Roman legions marched west to Bath and Bristol. A badger shied away from the campfires lit by the army of the luckless Duke of Monmouth, on the eve of his futile bid for the English crown. Throughout the blood-soaked annals of English history the badger has remained, living alongside man, yet secretly, apart, and though now driven back into the last tattered remnants of wilderness, he still survives.

On this moist February evening, Tobar foraged alone, for two days previously his mate, Mela, had retired to a small secluded chamber in an isolated corner of their underground home. Here, on a bed of dried fern and shriveled oak leaves, she had given birth to her cubs, and as yet Tobar had not been permitted to share the joys of parenthood with her. This was a familiar pattern in Tobar's life, for he was old, and had seen many litters raised by his mate.

He was old, and he was lean, for the long months of winter had taken their toll, and March, the hungry month, was yet to come. He still weighed over thirty pounds, and his yard-long body, built for strength rather than speed, was in no way weakened by the ordeal of winter. His gait was strong and purposeful, yet there was a curious rhythm to the pattern of his movement, for after every few strides, there came a check, a slight pause, as he stopped momentarily to listen.

In many ways Tobar resembled his American namesake. Both species have sturdy limbs, massively armed with strong black claws, and superbly adapted for digging. Both are shy and retiring, nocturnal in habit, but stubborn and fierce when roused. They share the same breeding pattern and diet, but the European badger is more catholic in his choice of food. In consequence, his premolar teeth are flattened, and he has four fewer than the American.

The European badger is slightly larger than his cousin, and his coat is grayer and coarser. He prefers to live in wooded hillsides, rather than open plains and prairies. His most distinctive feature, however, is his face. The American badger has a small, almost doglike face, with dark blotches on each cheek, and a thin stripe of white down the center of his forehead. The European badger's head is full and rounded, with wide cheeks and a high-domed forehead, tapering to a long, narrow snout, ending in a rounded boot button of a nose. The background color of his face and head is white, but starting about an inch from the tip of his nose, and running backward over the eyes and ears, are two broad black stripes, broken only by a white tuft at the tip of each ear.

Halfway down the hillside the woodland ended abruptly, to give way to arable land, a network of small fields, each bounded by thick hedgerows planted on top of a long earth mound, and bordered by a ditch, originally designed to drain the surplus water away from the fields. Many of these ditches had now fallen into disuse, and lay choked with leaves, weeds, fallen branches, and other debris.

These ditches were a favorite hunting ground for Tobar and his kind. He shuffled slowly along, his questing snout finding an earthworm here and there, an odd acorn overlooked by the pigeons the previous autumn, and now and again, in the mound beside the ditch, the sweet bulbs of wild hyacinth, already putting forth their green shoots. These Tobar dug from the moist earth with his powerful forelegs, crunching them with noisy gusto before moving on in search of fresh delicacies.

His way across the fields led him down the length of the valley, and parallel with the wood that cloaked the hill for more than a mile, until at last he came to the sunken track that ran at right angles to his path. Ahead lay the gaunt gray dwelling known as Bidewell Farm, standing like a sentinel guarding the entrance to the valley. Away to the left the track led to a tiny cottage, nestling close to the hillside on the verge of the wood. To the right it snaked uphill, leading to the road in the valley beyond. Tobar turned right, and wandered up the hill.

The rain had ceased now, but dense clouds still overhung the hills, and the light of the moon was veiled, so that even the startling striped mask of Tobar's face was barely visible in the shadowless pit of the night. Yet his progress up the track was so noisy, as he scratched and snuffled along, that a hunting owl, perched high in the bare branches of an ash tree, watched him as he passed underneath, and deciding that there wasn't room for two night hunters on the track, flew to a haystack three fields away.

The rain that had fallen during the day still flowed in a muddy rivulet beside the track, and here Tobar found more earthworms, washed out of the bank and now drowning in the cold water. He picked out each one, for earthworms were one of his favorite foods, and when conditions were right, they formed a large part of his diet. These victims of the rain were something of a bonus, although Tobar knew from experience that they were often to be found along the track in wet weather. His main objective, however, lay some distance away, beyond the crest of the hill and across the road.

The road itself was at once an attraction and a danger to wildlife. Once it had carried little traffic other than that belonging to the local people, and was largely deserted at night. Then a new multi-laned highway was built a few miles to the north, and what had once been a quiet country lane became an access road to the highway, and traffic flowed in an almost unceasing stream for twenty-four hours a day.

Small game, such as rabbits and voles, were frequently killed by passing vehicles, and their corpses lay smeared across the tarmac, attracting the attention of scavenging magpies, rooks, and crows. Hedgehogs were also drawn to the feast, and since their reaction to danger was to curl up in a tight, prickly ball, they, too, fell victim to the automobile. Tobar himself was not averse to a little scavenging, but tonight his destination was a field that bordered the other side of the road.

The previous year the farmer had planted potatoes in this field, harvesting the crop in late autumn. Tobar had visited the field one night when the crop was half gathered, and had developed a liking for the sweet white tubers. Now, although the crop had been lifted, and the field prepared for resowing, many potatoes still remained, some lying on the surface and washed clean by the rain, and others buried a few inches deep in the soil.

Tobar hesitated a long while before he crossed the road. The roar of the traffic bewildered him, and the glare of headlights, to eyes little accustomed to anything brighter than the dim light of the woodlands, was painful in the extreme. Nevertheless, he persisted, loitering on the verge of the road and waiting for a lull in the traffic. When it came he hurried across, and within seconds he had found and eaten his first potato.

An hour passed, and at the end of it Tobar was replete. By now the volume of traffic had lessened somewhat, and Tobar slipped through the hedge at a bend in the road. A heavy truck was climbing the hill. Tobar could hear the deep roar of its engine in the distance, but as yet it seemed a long way away. He did not know, as he set off across the road, that a fast sports car was coming down the hill.

It accelerated around the bend as he reached the center of the road, seeming to leap toward him as if to pin him to the ground with the twin beams of its headlights. Instinctively he turned away from the glare, and began running down the road, straight into the path of the oncoming truck. For a brief moment the world seemed ablaze with blinding light, and filled with the thunderous clamor of the diesel engine. Then he felt a heavy blow across his back, and there was nothing but a dark, empty void. The truck driver, dazzled by the lights of the other vehicle, had not seen the badger pass between his front wheels. He felt a slight jar as his rear wheel struck something, and then forgot it as the truck roared on into the night.

Tobar regained consciousness almost immediately, and made a desperate effort to stand, to regain the sanctuary of the field. He was unable to rise. His back was broken, his hindlegs trailing and useless. Slowly he hauled himself forward by his forelegs, his claws slipping and scrabbling on the smooth tarmac. He was bleeding from a dozen internal injuries, and though he felt no pain, his strength was ebbing fast. He reached the hedge, and gasping for breath, hauled himself through, to roll into the ditch beyond.

It was his last act. At the moment of his death the clouds parted, and a single star shone down. For an instant in time it sparkled, reflected in Tobar's eye, but then the star moved in the heavens, and its light was gone. Hidden in the undergrowth, the body of Tobar began to settle back into the earth from which it came, and all was one with the night and the silent stars.

2. The Heir to Summercombe

Deep in the darkness of the hill, Mela the sow badger groomed her solitary cub. Originally she had given birth to three, but one had failed to draw breath, and another had a heart deformity, so that its awakening brain was deprived of vital oxygen. On the second night of its life it slipped into a coma from which there was no awakening. The third cub, Borun, proved to be a fat and lusty infant, and since from the beginning he was assured of a more than ample supply of nourishment, he showed promise of becoming an exceptionally robust boar.

As soon as the bodies of the other cubs had grown cold, Mela had eaten them, clearing away their remains in the same fastidious manner she had disposed of the afterbirths. It may be that she felt no grief, or sense of loss, and perhaps without their soft, squirming embrace, without the sound of their infant voices to invoke mother love, they were of no interest to her. Instead, she concentrated on the living.

Borun was about four and a half inches long when he was born, and weighed three ounces. His short fur was a dirty white, and as yet the prominent black stripes of his face were but faintly etched, in mere suggestion of a design. He was blind and toothless, and totally dependent on his mother.

About an hour before dawn, Mela left him snug in his deep bed of fern, and slipped out of the nursery. Her sojourn outside was brief. She visited first the latrine, a series of small open pits screened by elder thickets, in a part of the woodland the badgers had set aside for this purpose. Then she moved off through the wood, following a wide, well-worn track that led to where a small spring bubbled out from beneath a limestone outcrop. Here she drank deep, and then, as if in sudden fear that her cub might be in danger, she hurried back to her nest.

Time passed. She slept a little, fed Borun, and meticulously groomed him, washing his plump, wriggling body with long strokes of her smooth, pink tongue. As the hours drifted by she began to grow increasingly uneasy, for she felt sure that her mate had not returned. She should have heard his purring call of greeting as he passed by the nesting chamber on his way to his own quarters. Even if she had been asleep she would have awakened to his call, and if he had returned while she had been at the spring they would have met, for the badgers' last act before retiring was to drink. Now the day was well advanced, and she was at a loss to understand his absence. Although the nest chamber had two exits, each discreetly hidden in the undergrowth, it did not connect in any way with the main network of tunnels that were mined into the hill. Shortly before dusk fell, Mela again left the nursery.

The evening was fine, but a cold wind from the north sent ragged black clouds racing over the crest of the hill, and the upper branches of the trees sighed and groaned. Mela stood in an amphitheater of bare, trodden earth. Above her were the dark openings of her citadel. The badgers made no attempt to disguise the whereabouts of their earth, or set, as it was called. Seven holes were visible, three at the base of trees, and one led deep under a rock. The others were mere holes in the sloping ground, and while some were quite small, so that it did not seem possible that a badger could squeeze down them, others were so large that it would be quite possible for a grown man to crawl inside. At the entrance to each hole a great mound of earth bore testimony to the mining activities that had taken place inside the hill. Over the years the badgers had excavated hundreds of tons of earth and small stones, and indeed the arena in which Mela stood was paved with the yellow sandy subsoil, some of it dug out centuries ago.

Mela went straight to an entrance beneath a great oak tree, where she and Tobar had last shared quarters before the birth of her cubs. Immediately inside the entrance the tunnel turned right, passing between the oak's roots, which now moved slightly as the wind swayed the tree. She was in darkness now, but she moved with the assurance of one long familiar with the layout of the tunnel, now dipping down, now squeezing flat to pass beneath a mighty rock whose base formed the roof of the tunnel. Thus she came to the sleeping chamber, but the bedding was cold, and the scent of her mate was stale on the crushed bracken fern.

She moved on, to a point where the tunnel forked, and emerged into the open from beneath the rock. Systematically she explored the whole set. It took her a long time, and at the end of her search she remained disquieted.

Meantime she was aware of other, more urgent needs. She was both hungry and thirsty, and it was now quite dark. First, however, she went to check on her cub.

Borun was lost to the world in warm, milky slumber. Mela withdrew silently, without waking him. Outside the wind was rising still, blowing almost to a full gale, but the woods and valley were sheltered from its main force. Stray gusts of wind tugged at the tops of the tallest trees, and ruffled the hair on Mela's back as she moved out of the woods and into the fields. The wind, and the light of the moon as it shone fitfully through the scudding clouds, had a curious effect on the badger's appearance. One moment she looked dark, almost black, and then the next minute she appeared to be as white as her newborn cub.

The explanation lay in the coloring of her hair. Each long hair on her back and flanks was white at the tip, for about a third of its length. The middle third was dark brown, almost black, but the lower third, to the root, was again white. So, as the wind disarranged the even lay of her hair, she seemed to change color, and from time to time she merged so successfully with the shadows of the night that she was completely invisible.

Almost at once she was lucky in her foraging. A mole, burrowing among the grass roots in search of earthworms, came so close to the surface that it made the ground heave. Instantly Mela pounced, tearing at the turf to expose the tunnel and thrusting her long snout into the cold, damp earth. Next moment the luckless mole was seized from behind and dragged out into the open.

Mela devoured her victim completely, skin, fur, and bones, even the tough, spadelike forefeet. Then she moved on, not daring to linger lest she should leave her cub unprotected for too long, although there was little danger from other predators. Stoats and weasels had too much respect for the size and strength of their cousin the badger, and even a fox was unlikely to venture into the set as long as her scent was fresh around the entrance. The chief danger to Borun was that of chilling, for he was not yet old enough or active enough to keep himself warm.

She snatched a few mouthfuls of grass, and behind the bark of a rotting tree stump she discovered a small colony of hibernating snails. Then she dug a quantity of wild hyacinth bulbs from the hedge bank. In doing so she found several earthworms and the fat white grub of a cockchafer beetle. Her hunger satisfied, she hurried back to the set. The cloud had thickened, and flurries of snow were beginning to fall.

Borun woke as she entered the nest chamber and burrowed blindly to her side, thrusting his nose at her flank and kneading her with eager paws. Relaxing, she let him feed, and fell into a half doze, while outside the snow continued to fall, drifting in the strong northerly wind.

It snowed all night, and for most of the following day, but by nightfall the blizzard had passed. The wind died, and the moon shone over a white and silent world. Mela emerged briefly, but finding she was still alone, returned to the warmth and shelter of the nursery. At times like these there was nothing to do but sleep, and conserve energy. Like all her kind she had an infinite capacity for slumber, and although the reserves of fat she had accumulated the previous autumn were now dwindling, she could readily draw upon them for a few days without suffering any inconvenience. A few mouthfuls of snow, snatched up on one of her infrequent visits to the latrine, were sufficient to quench her thirst.

For three days and nights the frost held. In the bright moonlight the rabbits emerged from their burrows, to flounder through the snow and gnaw the bark of young hazel shoots. Some died, caught in the jaws of the lean red foxes that lay in ambush among the snowdrifts.

Beneath the snow, through a maze of tunnels and passageways that formed an intricate network between the stems and roots of the rough herbage, weasels harried the mice and voles, while the white owl floated in vain over the fields, and was eventually forced to compete with the farmyard cats around the rickyards, where the rats and mice robbed the farmer of his grain.

Then the wind rose again, this time from the south, blowing wet and warm and bringing rain to wash the snow away. The thaw brought relief to the disconsolate flocks of fieldfares and lapwings, but for two days life was a torment of shivering, sodden misery to the small creatures of the grasslands, who woke to find their homes and highways flooded with icy water. Then the sun shone, the blackbird sang his territorial song for all concerned to hear, and the tide of spring flowed once more.

Each year the pattern was the same, for the land lay on the western border of a huge continental land mass. High pressure over the continent brought fine weather and clear skies to Britain, hot in summer, cold in winter, but these high-pressure systems were continually in conflict with depressions and troughs of low pressure from out in the Atlantic, and the tide of victory ebbed and flowed. So, as the earth tilted on its axis, and the hours of daylight slowly lengthened, each living thing, moss and fern and grass and gnarled old oak, waited its time, and when the temperature rose sufficiently high, responded in growth. Each time the temperature dropped, growth ceased, but the advance of spring, though slow and hesitant, was sure, until at last it swelled forward on a running tide that could not be stemmed.

Snug in the confines of the set, Borun continued to thrive. His eyes opened on the eleventh day, and at a month old he was exploring the confines of the nursery. His mother left him on most evenings, but never for long periods, and usually while he slept. As he grew older and stronger he spent hours playing and wrestling with her, tugging and pulling at her hair and trying to nip her with his baby teeth. Mela bore the torment with good humor, seeming to realize instinctively that the exercise was vital for his development and growth.

He got his first glimpse of the outside world on a fine warm evening in the middle of April. For some days he had shown signs of restlessness, of an eagerness to explore, and on several occasions he had left the nursery and crept hesitantly along the tunnel to the point where it forked. Each time his nerve had then failed him, and he had scuttled back to the safety of the nest. On this night his mother left him as usual, only to return after about ten minutes and nose him gently out of the chamber and along the tunnel. So he emerged, to sniff the sweet-scented air of spring and to sit trembling with mingled fear and excitement, secure between the stout forelegs of his mother.

Mela was equally nervous and apprehensive, and after about ten minutes she drove him underground, but the next night he stayed out longer, and made several short exploratory dashes around the mouth of the set, returning panting to his mother's side. Each night he grew a little bolder, a little more venturesome, while she stayed at the mouth of the set, growling a warning only if in her opinion he strayed too far.

She seemed to have wholly forgotten about her mate, and indeed she had long since ceased to look for him, but from time to time half-forgotten memories of him returned, and she found herself waiting to hear the pad of his feet on the path or the purring call of his greeting at the mouth of the set.

Once, as she was crossing the dew-drenched valley in the gray light of an April dawn, she heard the distinctive pad of feet that heralded the approach of another badger, and she stopped still, waiting as he came into view from behind a hawthorn thicket. She whickered a call of greeting, for she was sure that it was Tobar. Then she realized her error. The badger was a stranger, and he stood aloof, disinterested, respecting her sex and her right to be present, but offering no friendship. After a moment she moved on, and the young boar, a bachelor, returned to his own set, which he had dug in an old rabbit warren on the other side of the valley to the wood.

3. Woodland Childhood

In the weeks that followed, as spring matured into full-leafed summer, Borun grew in strength, stature, and wisdom. Each evening as the sun set and the last light of day lingered beneath the trees, he emerged from the stuffy confines of the set, a small, snub-nosed replica of his mother, to breathe air fragrant with the perfume of green growth. The sharp smell of moss, the spicy aroma of sun-warmed earth, the pungency of crushed fern, blended with a thousand other scents, stimulated and intoxicated him, and the pent-up energy within him exploded in a wild capering romp, a headlong gallop around the arena, up and down the worn paths, in and out of the bushes, until at last he collapsed at his mother's side.

During this outburst Mela was content to relax, to scratch

and groom herself, and enjoy the luxury of lying stretched out, limbs asprawl, in the cool evening air. Then, when the first wave of exuberance had passed, and Borun had sobered down a little, the serious business of his education could begin.

She led him along the ancient badger highways that criss-crossed the wooded hillside, taught him to use the latrine, and showed him the spring that bubbled out from beneath the limestone outcrop. He learned how to dig for wild hyacinth bulbs, and how to locate the fat white cockchafer grubs that lay hidden among the grass roots. She encouraged him to rip the bark from rotten tree stumps in search of beetles and woodlice, and showed him where the bank voles built their nests.

Each night he learned something new: how to de-slime a slug by rolling it on the ground with his forepaws, and how to catch earthworms as they lay outstretched on the short, sheep-bitten turf of the pastures, stalking them as they glinted in the starlight and snapping them up before they had time to withdraw into their burrows. Best of all, she taught him how to find young rabbits.

Rabbits swarmed everywhere in the valley, honeycombing the banks and hedgerows with their burrows, and robbing the farmer of his grass. Some years previously they had been virtually wiped out by a virus disease called myxomatosis, artificially introduced into Britain from the continent, but a few individuals remained immune, and from these survivors the rabbits began once again to populate the land. Since in favorable conditions rabbit does could produce a litter of five or six young every month from January to June, their numbers were soon restored. Five rabbits together consumed as much grass as one sheep, so they were not popular with the farmers on whose land they lived.

Before the arrival of her litter, each doe rabbit dug a short, blind burrow on the edge of the warren, scooping out a nest chamber at the end of the tunnel and lining it with fur plucked from her own breast. Here she could raise her young in secrecy, and if she left the burrow for any reason, she would block the entrance against the danger of a marauding weasel or stoat.

Many of these nest chambers lay close to the surface of the soil. Mela taught Borun to listen for the muffled squeaking of the young, and to sniff out the strong scent that rose up through the turf. Whenever they located such a nest, Mela dug down, tearing away the turf with her powerful claws, and scratching away the soil until she broke through into the nest chamber. Then, as the terrified mother fled, the helpless infants were snatched from the warmth of their nest and devoured on the spot. Borun always grew intensely excited on these rabbiting expeditions, so keenly did he appreciate the flavor of milk-fed rabbit, and tried hard to help with the digging. He was as yet more of a hindrance than a help, but his small forearms grew stronger as the weeks passed.

The badgers were true opportunity feeders, ready to sample anything that came within reach of their questing snouts. From time to time they came upon birds' nests containing eggs or young, and these they ate, as they did the fledglings that were unlucky enough to fall from the nest. They also ate snakes and frogs when they were to be found, and this caused Borun to make a tactical error, when one night he caught a toad between his jaws. The secretions from the toad's warty skin burned his gums and tongue, and caused him to shake his head in anger and irritation. The toad crawled safely away, and thereafter Borun was careful to avoid them.

On another occasion Borun made a more serious mistake, when he happened on a nest of leverets. Hares were scarce in the valley, and Borun did not know that while a mother rabbit might flee in terror, an angry mother hare was made of sterner stuff. As Borun ran at the leverets, he was knocked sideways by a resounding blow across the ear. Even as he tried to recover he was kicked again and again, and if his mother had not come to his rescue by distracting the hare and drawing her attention away from him, he might have suffered serious injury. Much chastened, he fled, and the hare abandoned her wild, leaping attack and returned to her young.

By preying on the rabbit population, and by cleansing the fields of the voracious cockchafer grubs that ate the grass roots and sometimes swarmed in such numbers that they threatened to destroy the pastures, the badgers were unwittingly helping the farmers whose fields they roamed. Yet because they went about their affairs in secret, and at night, their efforts went largely unnoticed. More evident was the occasional damage they inflicted, as when they wrecked a hedge bank in pursuit of rabbits, and so allowed stock to stray into adjacent fields.

Equally tactless was their habit of flattening growing cereal crops. Both Mela and Borun savored the sweet milky grains of young wheat and oats, and Borun could never resist romping and rolling through the stalks. His high spirits sometimes infected Mela, so that she played with him, and between them, in a very short space of time, they could flatten quite a large area. The loss to the farmer was not serious, but it was irritating, and gave the badgers a bad name, one that was not wholly justified.

For much of the time, however, the badgers limited their foraging to the wood. From a distance the wood looked like a cloak, flung carelessly asprawl the shoulder of the hill, extending for about a mile, and in places it was perhaps a quarter mile deep, a tiny fragment of the vast deciduous forests that had spread across southern England following the retreat of the last ice age.

It had survived for two reasons—the slopes of the hill were too precipitous and rock strewn to make it worth while attempting to clear the land for pasture, and until comparatively recent times, woodland was an important asset to any estate. Wood was needed for a multitude of purposes, from faggots for kitchen stoves to charcoal for blast furnaces, from floorboards to rafters for house and barn. Timber was needed for farm wagons and fence stakes, doors and window frames, handles for tools, chairs, tables, and beds. The newborn child was laid in a cradle of carved wood, and the old made their last journey to the grave in a rough-hewn coffin of oak or elm.

For many centuries most of this wood had to be found on or near the estate, so that although the woodland had survived the attentions of man, it had not escaped unharmed, and the marks of his handling were still to be traced.

At one time the woods had been as carefully managed as any other growing crop. Certain species of tree, such as oak and ash, were highly prized for their straight-grained, strong timber and good burning properties. Groves of hazelwood were cropped in the winter, and the smooth, straight rods were split and made into hurdles, portable sections of fencing to give shelter to the sheep at lambing time. Dead or decayed wood was cleared away, and scrub cut down to give light and air to the more valuable trees. In the autumn herds of pigs were allowed to graze through the woodlands, to grow fat on the acorns that fell from the oaks, and to fertilize the ground with their droppings.

Then came a period of abuse, with whole stands of trees cropped and sold as a commercial enterprise, until finally the woods were allowed to fall into disuse and neglect. Yet centuries would have to pass before the woods could return to their natural state. The hazel trees grew all awry, planted so close together that in competing for light they outgrew their root systems and fell, one against the other. From the boles of felled ash trees new growth pushed forth, so that throughout the woodland each massive base supported five, six, or seven tall trunks, each thicker than a man, and towering like gray-green spires to the sky.

Beneath the trees lay a jungle of twisted bramble and briar, from which sprang the climbing tendrils of honeysuckle and ivy, reaching out to the trees for support in their upward quest for light. Below the badger sets, in the soil spilled out over centuries of excavation, thickets of elder and nettle flourished so thickly as to inhibit any other form of growth.

The rich, moist leafmold of the woodland floor supported a host of flowering plants. First to flower were the tiny wood anemones, spilled like drops of congealed moonlight around the trunks of the trees. Then came the violets, in massed banks of purple, flanked by the green of their leaves. Primroses shone like pale yellow stars.

In May, as the cuckoo called and the swifts flew screaming over the meadows, the sunlit glades glowed with the blue haze of the wild hyacinths, their bell-shaped blossoms giving off a perfume so strong as to mask all others. In high summer the tangle of growth, of bracken fern and briar, was so tall that only the rosebay willow herb could tower above it, but the woods were sweet with the scent of the climbing honeysuckle and dog rose.

Unwanted and ignored by man, the woodland was in effect a focal point for the absorption of inspired energy. The damp leafmold, the yeasts and bacteria and fungi, the flowers and plants, the bees, wasps, and other insects, the mice and voles, the squirrels and birds and bats, all were so conjoined and interwoven as to become as one, and in the warm, heady stillness of a summer night this energy could be felt, as a soft, low vibration that was the pulse of the living earth.

The badgers were part of the pattern of woodland life, and while it might be said that the woodland was their domain, they were stewards rather than landlords, servants rather than masters. They were suffered, and their survival was guaranteed, only for so long as their energies were concentrated on creation rather than destruction.

If at times it seemed that the badgers were dedicated to a

lifetime of demolition, as when they wrecked a rotting tree stump in search of grubs or beetles, when they dug up wild hyacinths before they had a chance to flower, or when they tore open a vole's nest, spilling out the naked young and munching them up like soft-centered candies, then this was illusion. Such behavior, wanton and wasteful though it might appear, aided and assisted in the recycling of the elements of life, so that life, in all its myriad forms and bewildering complexity, could be reborn, fresh and new, over and over again.

By the middle of June, when Borun was four months old, he knew every inch of the woodlands, and had met all his neighbors, including the old dog fox that slept all day on a redolent bed of fern in a hollow ash stump at the top of the wood. If the wind was in the right direction Borun could smell the soft-footed old hermit coming long before he heard him. The badgers always gave him a wide berth, not because they were afraid of him but because, through no fault of his own, he offended their fastidious senses.

Occasionally the badgers ventured right across the wood, to where a small cottage stood at the end of a rutted track, in a small walled clearing amid the trees. Mela always seemed unduly nervous as they approached the clearing, and when Borun wanted to explore closer she drove him back. Many years ago Mela had been chased from the cottage by a pack of terrier dogs, and though the cottage had now changed hands, and the terriers long since departed, she had not forgotten the terror of that flight through the darkened wood.

The new owner of the cottage did have a pet though, and Borun met him on a hot windless night toward the end of June, as he padded quietly past the dwelling. The meeting was sudden. Borun rounded a bend in the path, and there, not a yard away, its back toward him, sat a half-grown, pure white tomcat. It was crouched, ready to spring on something about to emerge from the undergrowth, and for a moment the cat was unaware of the badger's approach. Then he turned, arched his back, and spat, and when Borun, in the short-sighted manner of his kind, took a couple of paces forward, the cat sprang into a tree and glared down at him. Borun was intrigued and puzzled, and would have liked to linger, but within seconds his mother was behind him, nervous as ever, and hustling him down the path. Borun cast a lingering look back, and the cat, which had settled itself comfortably on a branch, paws folded beneath it, yawned, and blinked complacently.

Mela led Borun out of the wood and down the hill, crossing several fields until they came to a narrow sunken track that ran the length of the valley, and gave access to the pastures that lay on either side. High banks, clothed with rank herbage, bordered the track, and Borun forgot the cat as he foraged for the fat black beetles that lumbered awkwardly among the plant stems.

A rattle of stones startled him, and he turned to see his mother attacking the top of the earth bank. She was clearly in a high state of excitement. The coarse hair on her back stood out at right angles, making her appear twice as large as normal, and as she dug she gave vent to a series of high-pitched grunts and squeals. A small flock of sheep stood bunched together at the far end of the field, watching, half fearful, half curious, as she sent showers of earth and large stones thudding down onto the track. Borun clambered up to join her, but she ignored him, and since he could see nothing that could justify the expenditure of such energy he grew bored, and wandered away.

The bank had been built almost a century ago, of stones loosely piled together, packed with soil, and thatched with turf. Thus secured, it had withstood the ravages of wind and rain for season after season, but it could not long withstand a determined assault by a badger. When Borun returned the bank was down, the lane partly blocked by rocks and soil, and Mela had uncovered her prize.

It was a large ball made from some papery, brown substance, and several black and yellow insects buzzed around it in sleepy, stupefied fashion. Mela broke open the ball, to reveal row after row of fat white grubs, and once Borun had tasted them, he understood why Mela had gone to so much trouble to unearth them, for to a badger there is no greater delicacy on earth than a wasps' nest.

The badgers finished their feast, and after lingering awhile to root about among the scattered fragments of the nest for any grub that might have been overlooked, they moved off into the night. An hour later the sheep, led by an old ewe, filed out of the field through the gap dug by Mela, and made off down the lane.

4. The Runaways

For Mr. Fletcher, of Bidewell Farm, the day started as on any other morning. Quite unaware that he had suffered any loss, he went about his routine tasks, milking his small herd of Friesian cows, tending to his pigs, and feeding the suckler calves that bawled their impatience from the old stable he had converted into a rearing pen. So it was not until after breakfast that he took his stick and walked up the lane that led to the valley.

Two miles away in the opposite direction, old Miss Ponsonby paused in the act of dressing to glance out her bedroom window. What she saw caused her to utter a shriek of dismay and hurry downstairs to the kitchen. Seizing a broom, she charged out the back door and into the vegetable garden, where a small flock of sheep were browsing contentedly on her lettuces. She was an agile and energetic old lady, and the sheep, panicking under the fury of her onslaught, scurried bleating out onto the road. Miss Ponsonby firmly latched the gate, and then, since she was not yet properly attired to appear in public, she hastened back indoors. She had just gained the sanctuary of her kitchen when she heard the high-pitched hornet whine of young Tommy Thornbeare's motor-bike coming down the lane, and she heaved a sigh of relief that he had not arrived on the scene a few seconds earlier.

Tommy Thornbeare's great love in life was his shiny new Japanese two-stroke. He had twice failed to pass his driving test, but he was convinced that his lack of success was due to prejudice on the part of the examiners, and was in no way a reflection of his driving skill, which he rated high. Now, as he flung the machine into a bend, he saw himself crouched low over the handlebars, leading the field in some motorcycle Grand Prix. The next instant he found himself floundering in a sea of wool.

The sheep were all over the road, galloping at breakneck speed, but Tommy was going faster. Miraculously, he passed through the flock without causing a single casualty, although all the while he was skidding and lurching and fighting for control of his machine. There remained one old ewe out in front, and it seemed to Tommy that his front wheel was drawn to her like a magnet. The wheel butted her none too gently from behind, and with an indignant bleat, the ewe darted off at a tangent. Tommy went straight on, over the handlebars of his bike, and through the hedge, where he lay paralyzed with shock and fright, as the bleating of the sheep faded in the distance.

At first Tommy was convinced that every bone in his body was broken, so he was surprised, and even a little disappointed, to discover that he was in fact unhurt. Nor was his machine damaged, but his bright red crash helmet was scratched, and his yellow plastic jacket was torn beyond repair. Thoroughly out of humor, he remounted his machine and rode off, this time at a more sedate pace, determined to find the owner of the sheep and sue him for damages.

The owner was at that moment staring with horror at the empty field where his sheep should be. The flock which was missing was a very special one, one which he had recently spent a great deal of money to acquire. They belonged to an ancient breed known as the Ryeland, very hardy and resistant to disease, producing high-quality meat and yielding heavy fleeces of soft fine wool. With them he hoped not only to make a handsome profit, but to gain prestige by exhibiting them at the various agricultural shows. Now he had lost them.

At first he thought he had been the victim of sheep rustlers, for a gang had been known to operate in the district, but then he found the gap in the hedge. For a moment or two his feeling was one of relief, that the sheep were not stolen, but strayed, but then he found the remains of the wasps' nest, and his anger grew as he recognized the identity of the culprit. Hurrying back to the farm, he flung open the door. "The Ryelands have gone," he shouted.

Mrs. Fletcher appeared from the kitchen, drying her hands on her apron. "Gone? What do you mean, gone?" she queried.

"Strayed, of course. Broken out of the field and gone. Heaven knows where they are now, or how I'll get them back again."

Mrs. Fletcher sniffed. She had never entirely approved of her husband's lifelong obsession with sheep. They brought more plague than profit, in her opinion, and buying this latest lot of Ryeland ewes had seemed to her an act of extreme folly. "You want to spend more time with your fences if you want to keep fancy sheep," she remarked tartly. "I've said before that they are a disgrace to the farm."

Fletcher's eyes bulged and his neck reddened. He was a

big blond man with shambling limbs and powerful, work-worn hands, normally placid and easygoing, but at times like this rage made him inarticulate. He found his tongue at last. "It was a badger, you stupid woman. A badger dug out a wasps' nest and broke down the bank. I'll have him directly. In fact, if anything has happened to those ewes I'll kill every badger in the county."

Mrs. Fletcher was in no way cowed by his anger. "Perhaps you'd be better employed looking for your sheep, than standing there bellowing," she remarked. "Take the dog and be off. I've got my own work to do."

Still grumbling, Fletcher turned on his heel, but at that moment the telephone rang. Mrs. Fletcher picked up the receiver, and then called to her husband. "It's for you. Seems Mrs. Applecross has found your sheep."

In two strides Fletcher was at the telephone. "Where are they?" he snapped.

"Why, in Major Fuller's orchard," replied Mrs. Applecross. "I was just looking out across the valley . . ."

She was left talking to herself. Fletcher was racing for his Land Rover, and shouting instructions to Mrs. Fletcher to call Major Fuller and ask him to hold the sheep. As he drove away he was wishing that his flock had chosen somewhere else to stray. Major Fuller was a magistrate, and a stickler for law and order. He was also of uncertain temperament, and he was quite likely to impound the sheep until Fletcher could prove ownership, and then charge him for their keep.

He need not have worried. Major Fuller, less red in the face and peppery than usual, met him at the gate. "Sorry, Fletcher," he barked. "Lost 'em. My dog drove them off just before your wife phoned. They'll be right down in the village by now."

Fletcher groaned and crashed the Land Rover into gear. The day was not working out at all well. He finally ran his sheep to ground in the churchyard, where they were grazing placidly among the tombstones, and stubbornly resisting the somewhat half-hearted efforts of the verger to drive them out. The flock was by now thoroughly unsettled, and reluctant to move in the heat of the day, so Fletcher had to abandon his Land Rover and walk in front of the flock, all the way back to the farm, while his dog brought them on from behind. On the way he had a painful interview with Miss Ponsonby, who had been lying in wait for him, and then he met the village constable, who told him with some relish about the adventures of young Tommy Thornbeare.

It was a depressed and weary man who finally penned his sheep securely in a field close by the farmhouse. Although, legally, he could not be held responsible for the damage caused by his straying flock, he still had to live with his neighbors, and he had managed to upset quite a few. Somehow he would have to make amends. At the back of his mind, too, was the fear that while they were free the sheep might well have eaten something that would upset them. He reflected grimly that if they had eaten as much fresh greenstuff as Miss Ponsonby had claimed, they would all be down with colic by now.

Meanwhile, he still had to collect his Land Rover from where he had abandoned it, and there was work on the farm which could not be left for the morrow.

It took him the greater part of the following day to repair the damage done by Mela to the earth bank. After a day of hard labor and smoldering resentment under the hot sun, he took a walk round his fields, noting several places where the badgers had pushed through the hedge and slid down the earth bank. His Ryeland ewes were secure in their field, and seemed to have suffered no ill effects from their outing. All the same, a long hot summer lay ahead, and there were bound to be many more wasps' nests in the banks. Fletcher felt he could not risk further disaster. The next day was market day, and he took time to visit the ironmongers in the town.

5. Fletcher's Revenge

The weather continued hot and dry, with little or no dew at night. Instead, a warm breeze drifted over the land, keeping the night air warm, so that the moisture that had transpired from the earth during the day was carried high into the sky, instead of condensing on the ground. The pastures were arid and brown, and the earthworms lay deep in their burrows, each tightly coiled in a ball to conserve moisture.

Borun and Mela now emerged from the set in full daylight, to forage through the leafy stillness of the wood. All bird song had now ceased, save for the monotonous call of the wood pigeons and the occasional raucous scream of a jay. In spite of the drought, and the hard-baked earth, that made digging a laborious and often futile task, the badgers continued to feed well. Nests of young rabbits were still plentiful, and formed a major part of the badgers' diet at this time. In addition, there were cockchafers, fat brown beetles that droned through the air in clumsy, laborious flight, and pitched on the ground with an audible thump that never failed to attract the badgers' attention. The cockchafers laid their eggs in pasture, where the larvae remained for three years, eating the grass roots. From time to time the cockchafers occurred in such numbers as to destroy whole fields, but the badgers helped to keep them in check, eating adults and larvae with equal gusto.

Always there were mice and voles. Left to themselves, the voles alone would destroy the world. Although each weighed less than an ounce, a vole could eat its own weight in dry matter in ten days, and there could be as many as five hundred voles to the acre in neglected grassland. Such a heavy population, if it remained constant, would eat the equivalent of half a ton of hay in a year, but if the population was allowed to grow unchecked it would multiply tenfold in six months, and long before the end of the year would have consumed more than ten tons of vegetable matter, more than the most fertile acre could produce.

It was now high summer, and the vole population was at its peak. Every female was pregnant, and each was raising a litter of five or six young. In three weeks' time she would have weaned that litter, and be giving birth again, while the survivors of her first brood, if any, would be fast approaching maturity. Fortunately, few voles lived longer than six months, and not one in a thousand survived for more than a year.

The remainder got eaten, devoured by foxes, cats, stoats, weasels, hawks, crows, owls, herons, and jays. Grass snakes and adders took them from their nests, birds harried them by day and night, and even the fat old toad took an occasional infant if it ventured too close. It was as though some supreme intelligence had taken the cellulose and undigestible carbohydrate of the field and processed it through some vast factory, turning out the vole as a prepackaged survival ration, not too big or too small, containing all the essential ingredients, blood, bone, fur, and meat, in an easily available form. The very name vole is Old English for field, and this was what the voles were, a living, moving, hot-blooded field on which the predators could graze. As a final touch of genius, it was ordained that the supply would be available for twenty-four hours a day, for the vole divided each day into two-hour periods of activity, with short rests in between.

With such a surfeit of food, Borun developed rapidly. He was now almost half grown, and quite able to forage for himself, but badgers are sociable animals, and Borun still felt the need for companionship and security. So mother and son continued to keep each other company on the nightly forage, returning together to the set in the cool milky light of the dawn.

Gradually, however, a change was coming over Mela. She felt irritable and frustrated, frequently impatient of Borun and intolerant of his demands to share whatever food she found. Quarrels were frequent, and on occasions Borun got sharply nipped for importuning too persistently.

Mela did not understand what was happening to her. She could not know that the radiation of the sun, the moon, and the stars, the tilting of the earth on its axis, its position in the planetary system, all were conspiring with the chemistry of her glands to send hormones coursing through her system. Mela, in short, needed a mate, for now was the honeymoon season of the badgers. Normally Tobar would have been around, but he had never returned, and the young boar across the valley had taken a mate of his own.

The fine spell ended at last, with low cloud obscuring the moon and a thin drizzle soaking gently into the dry earth. The earthworms, sensing the presence of moisture, climbed up their burrows to emerge into the night, and Borun and Mela fed well, for once without quarreling over the spoils.

Maybe it was her pleasure over the feast of earthworms, or maybe it was the pent-up desires still smoldering within her that made Mela careless. She ran down the hill, pushed through a gap in the hedge, and started to slide down the bank. Next moment she was held tight, by the constricting wire of a snare, set none too expertly by Fletcher a week ago, gripping her tightly around the waist. She hung head down, screaming with rage and pain, while Borun whimpered anxiously behind her.

The noose had been set too wide, or it would have caught her around the neck, strangling her as she fell. As it was, she was still alive, but trapped. She managed to claw herself around, and pull herself back onto the hedge bank, where she began to bite and tug at the roots and branches around her. She dug and fought and tore until her pads were broken and her claws torn, her gums bleeding and raw, but to no avail. The farmer had fastened the snare to the root of a gnarled old hawthorn, thicker than a man's arm, and so tough and strong that it would have held a bear.

Toward dawn she ceased to struggle, and lay exhausted, her coat matted with mud and sticky earth, mixed with blood and saliva. Borun had tried to help even to the point of trying to bite through the wire, but it had been twisted from many fine strands, and foiled every attempt to cut it. Now as he approached her she screamed and snapped at him, half mad with fear, and so at last he went and crouched down some distance away, afraid of her in her rage. Still he lingered, long into the gray daylight, while Mela lay amid the wreckage of the hedge, demolished in her struggles.

Footsteps, and a man's cough, alerted Borun. They drew nearer. His frayed nerves failed him, and he bolted. As he reached the sanctuary of the woods he was deafened by the blast of a shotgun.

Borun remained in the set throughout the day, and for most of the following night, emerging just before dawn and creeping fearfully, almost unwillingly, to the site where he had left his mother the morning before. The bank had been repaired, and the gap plugged with a bush of thorn, but Mela's body still lay in the ditch where Fletcher had thrown it. Borun approached cautiously, the hairs on his spine stiff and erect. He called, a low, hesitant greeting, but there was no response. Then he drew nearer, and sniffed around her corpse. Recognizing the smell of death, he turned away, and finally made his way slowly back into the woods. Ever after, he avoided going near the place.

Gradually, in the days that followed, he began to forget about her, but often, in the evenings after the sun had gone down, in the lingering afterlight of summer, he would wander disconsolately about the set, pausing at each entrance in turn, listening, but hearing nothing but the silence of the hollow hill. At length he would turn away, padding doggedly down the worn trail to start another lonely night's foraging.

6. Vandal

Over the years the cottage seemed to have settled cozily into the side of the hill, so that now the thatch, made rotten by the moss that grew thick upon it, merged with the green canopy of the trees, and the weather-worn stone of the walls exactly matched the hue of the yellow sandy soil. Climbing tendrils of ivy, which had sent their suckerlike roots deep into the crevices between the stones, further obscured the outline of the cottage, so that from across the valley it was barely visible, except when a thin gray column of smoke rose from the chimney.

All day the sun had shone down on the garden, warming the rich, moist soil so that the serried ranks of vegetables, the peas and carrots and cabbages, the green-leaved lettuces, and the golden bulbs of the onions seemed to swell visibly by the hour. Now the sun was westering. As it passed behind the cottage, just before it slid beneath the crest of the hill, its rays penetrated a small casement window, and a beam of soft rosy light fell upon the sleeping form of a white cat, curled at the foot of the bed.

In response to the sun's caress, an ear twitched. The cat raised his head, opened his eyes, and yawned. Then he lay still as his senses alerted him to the pattern of his surroundings.

Almost at once he realized that something was wrong. There should have been the rich smell of cooking, but only the stale smells of yesterday lingered on the air. There should have been a scattering of tiny sounds, all significant, all related to the time of day. There was nothing, only the ticking of the clock in the living room, the faint creaking of timbers as the house cooled after the heat of the day, and an intermittent rustling in the roof as the bats beneath the thatch began to wake from their daytime sleep.

For a short while the cat, whose name was Vandal, remained on the bed, hoping at least to hear his favorite sounds, the rattle of a saucer and the rhythmic scrape of a can-opener cutting its way around the lid of a can, sure signs that a meal was ready. Vandal waited in vain, and eventually he slid off the bed, stretched, and made his cautious way downstairs.

The living room and the kitchen were deserted. The ashes of the fire were cold in the hearth, and the breakfast table lay uncleared. There was a thick package wedged in the letter slot in the front door, but nothing else. Vandal turned, and went back upstairs, to pause and scratch at the closed door on the landing. In the past this act had always evoked a response, though not always friendly. This evening it brought nothing.

Vandal returned to the kitchen. The situation was not entirely novel to him. In the past he had been left alone on several occasions, but each time there had been food left out for him, and milk in a saucer under the table. This time there were only the stale, sour remains of his breakfast, which after sniffing tentatively for a while he rejected, performing a ritual burial act with his paw on the tiled floor surrounding the plate.

Then he left the house. The kitchen door was closed and locked, but there was an ingenious device known as a cat-flap fixed in the lower panel of the door, through which he could come and go at will. Outside the air was cool and fresh, and heavy with the scent of elder flower and honeysuckle, but the fragrant beauty of the summer evening was wasted on Vandal. He moved away uphill, past the chickens bunched together in their pen, past the rabbit that stamped nervously in her hutch, over the loose stone wall, and into the wood. Blackbirds chinked angrily from the safety of their roosts in the elder thickets. A wood pigeon flew out with a clatter of noisy wings, making Vandal flatten his ears and spit in futile rage. He came at last to the badger track that ran athwart the hill, and followed it, pausing every now and then to listen, until he came at last to the edge of the wood, and the hedge that bordered the field.

Rabbits had emerged from their burrows, and begun to feed on the short, sheep-cropped turf of the field. In the afterlight their gray forms were clearly visible against the green of the grass. Vandal's teeth chattered in anticipation as the rich gamy scent reached him, and belly flat to the ground, he stole down the hedgerow to the shelter of a bramble patch.

The bramble patch, a seemingly impenetrable thicket of hawthorn, blackthorn, and wild briar rose, tightly interwoven with the heavily barbed growth of the brambles, was in fact honeycombed with tunnels cut by the rabbits themselves, and it was through this maze that the cat made his way, until at last he lay in ambush, hidden by the overgrowth, but with a clear view of the field, and of several young rabbits that were feeding upwind, and steadily moving nearer the thicket. Vandal, the events of the past few hours obliterated from his mind, waited for the moment to spring.

Three young rabbits were now within range. Though little more than a quarter grown, one would provide an ample meal. The cat took a quick glance around. The nearest full-grown rabbits were several yards away. There would be no danger of a humiliating and painful attack from an angry buck or protective doe.

Vandal's gaze returned to his prey. One young female detached herself from the group and hopped his way. Saliva filled his mouth as he sprang. The soft furry form squirmed beneath him as his teeth met in her neck. He felt the vertebrae part and the blood from her severed arteries flow into his mouth, heard vaguely the angry stamp of warning as the other rabbits bobbed away with flashing white tails, and then he was dragging his quarry back into the bramble thicket.

He fed then, starting at the head and crunching his way through bone, skin, fur, and sinew as well as the soft, succulent flesh, savoring the liver and heart but rejecting the stomach and entrails, until all else that remained were the hindlegs. Then he paused, satiated, and washed his feet as the fleas from the dead rabbit burrowed to safety in the short fur on his head. Replete and lazy, he sprawled out on the litter of dried grass and leaves beside the remains of his feast, and dozed off as the moon rose high in the sky and the rabbits reemerged, to feed on the dew-drenched grass. This time they gave the bramble thicket a wide berth.

When next the cat woke, the moon was still high in the sky, but now it was riding to the west, and already the eastern sky was silvered with the first light of dawn. The rabbits had deserted the field, and the air was chill. The cat stretched, making the time-honored obeisance of his kind, sniffed at the remains of the rabbit, and made a half-hearted attempt to finish them, but the flesh was cold and stiff, so he turned away, back toward the wood. Next morning a flesh fly found the remains of the rabbit, and laid her eggs on the meat. Her labors were in vain, for the following evening a foraging hedgehog found the carrion, and ate it with relish, eggs and all.

The cat made its way slowly back through the wood, turning aside once to drink the brackish water that had accumulated in the center of an ash stump. A few laps sufficed, not because the taste was alien to him, but because he required little in the way of moisture to quench his thirst. Dawn was breaking as he slipped through the cat-flap, to find the house as still and silent as he had left it. He curled up in his favorite place on the bed in the spare room, and though he roused himself several times during the day, no sound came to disturb the peace of the cottage.

That evening the sun woke him as usual, and again the alien silence greeted him as before, with one difference. The ticking of the clock had ceased. This time he did not bother scratching at the closed bedroom door, nor did he search for food. Instead he went straight out, and sat for a while watching the chickens, which, having heard the rattle of the cat-flap, had crowded in eager anticipation around the door of the hen run. All day they had scratched without reward at the bare earth of the run, seeking for some overlooked scrap of food. Now with empty crops they crooned hopefully, gazing with bright eyes toward the house.

Vandal lingered, enjoying the familiarity of their presence. He was just over half grown, and at an age when he still desired company, had not yet fully acquired the self-sufficiency and assurance that marked his kind. In his memory lurked half-forgotten images, the warm, silken flank that was his mother, the rough tongues and squirming bodies that were his litter brothers and sisters. Overlaid on these mind pictures were more recent recollections, of an ample lap clad in rough tweed, a billowing satin bosom, and an endearing voice that used to croon to him as he lay, full fed and half asleep, in front of the flickering light and warmth of the fire.

Without the reassurance of such a presence, he felt insecure, uneasy. So he sat on, in the company of the fowls, until darkness fell, and one by one the hens went to roost in the fusty darkness of their coop. Then, reluctantly, he moved away in search of his supper.

He leapt onto the wall and dropped down into a clearing among the fern, and at once the mystery of the night surrounded and captivated him, so that he forgot his earlier unease. The air was filled with soft, furtive sounds, a rustle in the dry leaves, a flurry of movement in the honeysuckle vines, a crashing far off, and once a thin, high scream that ended in a choking gasp. He moved cautiously but confidently along the badger track, a predator with little to fear, alone in a world in which he was superbly equipped to survive.

He killed quickly and fed. This time his prey was a short-tailed vole, sweet and succulent, but not bulky enough to induce in him the lethargy that followed gorging to capacity. So he moved on, and surprised yet another vole as she scurried toward her nest of dried grass. This time he played with his victim, tossing her in the air and allowing her to crawl a few feet toward sanctuary before clawing her back and patting her, soft-footed, around, until at last she died of fear and shock. When at last he was convinced that she would run no more, Vandal ate her, leaving only her stomach, which he cut neatly out with his teeth. Then, aroused by the squeaking that emanated from the nearby nest, he clawed out and ate the pink hairless young of the vole.

So the night passed, but with the coming of the dawn Vandal was once more drawn toward the comfort and safety of the cottage. He retraced his steps in the direction of the house, and had almost reached the wall when, rounding a bend in the path, he came face to face with Borun the badger cub.

The cat froze, and so did the badger. They stood in the moonlight, immobile, each waiting for the other to move first. For perhaps half a minute neither animal flinched, and then Borun sank down on one haunch, and scratched himself vigorously with his hindclaws. Even to Vandal it was clear that this gesture could in no way appear aggressive. In token of acknowledgment he licked the inside of his forepaw, and then groomed his chest. Then he sat down and waited for the badger's next move.

Borun nodded his head several times, peering at the cat with myopic eyes, and then advanced. As he drew nearer Vandal's nerve slowly began to crack, until at last he stood up, ready to flee or attack. Then Borun moved to one side, and slowly, as Vandal circled to keep facing him, the cub passed him by, and rejoining the track, trundled slowly out of view. Five minutes later the cat was back in the bedroom of the cottage, where, after a prolonged and vigorous grooming session, he fell asleep. From time to time his body twitched, as he dreamed about badgers, and the voles that scurried and squeaked in the silver-splashed shadows of the moonlit wood.

He woke suddenly, to the sound of vehicles being driven slowly up the track that led to the cottage. He heard the slamming of car doors, footsteps, and a hubbub of alien voices, and then he fled, out of the cottage and into the sanctuary of the woodshed, where he crouched behind a pile of logs. He waited a long while, and although he was tempted to creep out and make acquaintance with these humans, fear held him back.

Outside the front door of the cottage, the village policeman stood talking to the doctor, as attendants bore a white-shrouded burden to the waiting ambulance. "It was the postman who reported it. He didn't call yesterday, but this morning he noticed that a package he'd delivered the day before was still wedged in the letter slot. Seems the old girl got up as usual, fed the cat and had breakfast, and then felt unwell and went back to bed.''

The doctor nodded absently. He was late for his surgery and anxious to be away. ''There's a brother, I believe?''

''That's right,'' nodded the policeman. ''He lives down in the village. I'll call round and see him directly. Someone will have to come and see to the hens and so forth. I expect the cat's about somewhere too.''

''I expect he's taken to the woods by now,'' said the doctor. ''At least there's plenty of food about for him. The rabbits seem to have come back thicker than ever since the myxomatosis.''

One by one the vehicles departed, and once again the silence of the summer day hung heavily over the deserted cottage. Gradually the stuffy heat of the woodshed grew unbearable to Vandal, and at last he crept out. This time, however, he did not return to the bedroom, but sought the leafy green shade of the woods. So he did not hear the arrival of the old man who fed the hens and the rabbit. Nor did he know that on the tiled floor of the kitchen were a saucer of fresh milk and a plate of cat food.

7. Strange Company

The long summer day was well advanced when Vandal next woke. For a while he lay still, couched on a bed of dried leaves that filled the hollow of an old ash stump, listening as the sounds of the day gave way to those of the night. Somewhere the distant drone of a tractor coughed and died, and a dog barked briefly in the silence. The thin, dry bleat of a half-grown lamb scraped across the evening air, and as if in answer a crow called, once, twice, as he winged his solitary way across the wood. Then an owl cried, the low, wavering voice echoing down the aisles of darkness.

In response the woodland came alive with movement. Bats began to flicker black-winged between the tree trunks, and from the undergrowth came the busy sound of small teeth, a brief patter of feet, a scuffle, and a muffled squeak as two mice fought a lilliputian duel, their tiny tempers white hot with rage. The nightjar detached himself from his roost on the bare branch of an oak and flew off to circle the cattle that grazed in the meadow, hawking for the flies that swarmed around the beasts. The woodcock in the fern opened her eyes and flopped away, ghostlike among the trees, to probe for worms in the marshland at the bottom of the valley.

Vandal slipped from his perch and padded off through the shadows. A dormouse shredding bark from the honeysuckle vine for her nest saw him as he passed beneath her, and whisked her tail as she fled upward into the high branches. A bank vole caught his scent and froze in the shelter of a fallen branch as he passed by. A young rabbit feeding in a clearing among the fern was not so alert. Vandal sprang, and there was a brief flurry of movement, a flash of white fur, and the next moment Vandal was dragging his limp prey into the shelter of the bushes.

Half an hour later the cat lay sprawled beside the remains of his feast, his flanks heaving and distended. Vandal was rather more than comfortably full, and disinclined to action of any kind, so for the next hour he stayed where he was, licking the blood from his paws in a rather desultory fashion, until his supper had settled somewhat. Then he got up, to prowl aimlessly through the wood.

He was not disposed to hunt further that night, and thoughts of his comfortable couch on the bed in the cottage lured him to return. Yet he could not forget his unease at the empty silence of the house, and the sudden invasion of his privacy by so many strangers. It was as though the whereabouts of his sanctuary had suddenly been betrayed to aliens, and once exposed, its safety could no longer be depended upon. Nor could he expect any affection or companionship on his return, for somehow he knew that his mistress had left the cottage. So he wandered on, and eventually emerged onto the badger track at the exact moment that Borun joined it, fifty yards away.

So the two animals met again, for the third time in their lives. For a long while each stood stock still, waiting for the other to make the first move. Both animals were certain that they had nothing to fear from each other, both were young and immature, and each nursed in his heart a feeling of loss, of loneliness, and a desire for companionship. Slowly, infinitely slowly, Vandal crept nearer and nearer to Borun, who remained rooted to the spot. At last they touched noses.

There followed a tentative inquiry into each other's person, the pair circling around and sniffing each other carefully. Borun had little scent, for like all badgers he was scrupulously clean in his person and living quarters. Vandal, for his part, smelled strongly of rabbit, which may have puzzled Borun, but almost certainly endeared Vandal to him. Satisfied, Borun set off down the track, with Vandal dancing along behind him.

During that first night Vandal watched, intrigued, as Borun wrecked a rotten tree stump, ripping off the bark and scooping up the beetles and other insects that tumbled in all directions. He grew disinterested when Borun dug for roots and bulbs among the bracken fern, but brightened up when the badger found a vole's nest, pouncing on the fleeing mother while Borun demolished the young voles. Vandal killed the mother, but he was not interested in food, and willingly allowed Borun to take possession of his prize.

By dawn, they had invented a curious game of tag, in which Borun first rushed at Vandal, who sat as still as a statue until the very last moment, and then sprang high into the air, so that Borun shot headlong under him. Then Vandal chased Borun, cuffing him with his paws, but making sure his claws were never unsheathed. Borun, long used to far heavier blows than Vandal could deal, nevertheless squealed in pretended terror and turned somersaults in his efforts to avoid them.

The game ended with the coming of daylight. The two made their way to the spring and quenched their thirst, and then as of habit Borun returned to the set. Vandal hesitated outside the entrance for a moment, and then, as Borun's rather portly rump disappeared into the darkness, he followed. The bed of fern and leaves was crisp and comfortable, and Borun's warm flank was soft and reassuring. As the tractor in the valley grumbled into life for yet another day, as the nightjar returned to his roost on the oak branch, and the sun climbed high in the sky, the strange companions slept.

Gradually, in the days that followed, the pair worked out a scheme of coexistence that suited them both. Although Vandal easily adapted to nocturnal life, he preferred to hunt and kill alone, early in the evening before the sun had set and the countryside had become soaked with dew. His hunger satisfied, Vandal was content to accompany Borun on his foraging, and lend assistance when necessary. Often, when Borun emerged from the set, there would be a portion of rabbit, still warm, waiting for him, and this was most acceptable to the badger cub, who was still at times inexpert and bungling in his attempts to find food.

For much of the time Vandal also preferred to sleep alone. Catlike, he chose to change his sleeping quarters regularly, to bask in the sun of early morning and late evening, but to seek shade during the noonday heat. So he had a succession of sleeping places near the set, each chosen in relation to the position of the sun and the direction of the wind. Only when it rained did he join Borun in the set, and as the summer wore on this happened less and less. The water level in the lakes and reservoirs dropped, the ground cracked, and the once green pastures turned a golden brown.

Early on an August morning, as the sun shone again from a cloudless sky, and the wind rustled through the acres of ripe wheat, Vandal was roused from a half slumber by a distant high-pitched bark. The yapping was persistent, rising and falling on the breeze, but drawing nearer. Fully awake now, Vandal listened, folding his paws beneath him, but poised for instant action if need be.

A terrier had escaped just after dawn from the farm where it was kept to control the rats that swarmed around the rickyards. Once before it had escaped, by scratching and biting until it had chewed a hole through the bottom of the shed door. The farmer had nailed a wooden patch over the hole, and forgotten it, but the terrier had not. Every night, after it had been locked in the shed, it went to work on the patch, and every day the hot sun and the lack of rain aided the terrier in its efforts. The timber dried out, the nails loosened in their holes, and the patch warped until finally it fell free.

The terrier had one idea in mind, and that was to run wild among the hordes of rabbits that swarmed amid the hedgerows, and as he hunted and killed, and missed, and chased again, he slowly went silly with excitement, barking hysterically the while, and running from warren to warren, until at last he entered the wood.

Vandal lingered a split second too long. He saw the black and white form of the terrier coming up the badger trail, and slid from his bed of fern, making for the shelter of the set. The terrier spotted him, and with a joyous yelp, dived in pursuit. Vandal reached the mouth of the set with the terrier in close pursuit.

It was hard on his heels as he ran down the tunnel, to the airy main chamber under the oak tree, where Borun now slept. The badger woke to hear the sounds of pursuit, the scrabble of claws, and the snuffling bark of the dog. Next moment Vandal burst into the chamber, a split second before the terrier, and as the cat turned to face his adversary the dog leapt at him, aiming for the throat, but seizing him at the side of the neck, just below his ear. As Vandal screamed Borun leapt to attack, and with a sudden lurch of fear the terrier felt the badger's teeth sink into his foreleg.

In the darkness the noise and confusion were bewildering to all three contestants. The terrier yelled as Borun's teeth grated on bone, and Borun released his hold, leaping for the terrier's throat. He caught the dog instead behind the ears, holding it by the scruff of the neck and effectively preventing it from biting any more. The dog struggled frantically, shaking Borun around the chamber, and forgetting about Vandal, who had broken free when the terrier opened its jaws to yell.

Few dogs have ever been forced to endure the unbridled fury of an enraged tomcat, and those who have are reluctant to suffer the experience ever again. The terrier was within seconds of such a punishment, and there could be no reprieve. Vandal sprang at the dog, biting and slashing with razor-sharp teeth, all the while clinging to the dog's back with claws that gored deep. Finally he brought the powerful muscles of his hindlegs into action, raking the soft flanks of the terrier with the terrible back-raking kick that could disembowel a rabbit.

Between them, the companions might well have succeeded in killing the terrier, had it not, with one last effort, managed to reach the exit from the chamber, forcing its way into the tunnel and brushing the pair off. It crawled painfully back to the farm, where Fletcher, who had been prepared to give it a beating for straying away, could only look at it in wonder and dismay. He told his friends about it, in the public bar of the inn that evening. "Little old dog looked as though he'd been through a threshing machine. He's cut and tore and scratched, and I can't see how badly for caked blood. One drink of milk he's had, and laid like a dead thing ever since. What manner of beast could do that to him I can't imagine."

Nor, for that matter, could anyone else. The two assailants were little the worse for wear after their adventure. Borun had a few scratches, dealt him in error by Vandal in the height of the melee, and Vandal had a nasty tear in the side of his neck. Carefully, they administered first aid to each other, each licking those injuries the other couldn't reach, and their wounds healed without complication. The terrier recovered in time, but he never went near the wood again.

8. Polly and Her Guests

As soon as Polly saw the cottage she knew she had found the place she had been looking for. It was September, and the garden was derelict and weed strewn, but in her mind's eye she saw it well tended and trim, with serried rows of vegetables flourishing in the plump soil. There was a lawn, with a gnarled old damson tree. In the spring bulbs would force their green spears above the grass, first snowdrops, then crocuses, purple and yellow and white, and then daffodils, nodding in the wind and flaunting their golden trumpets in the thin March sun. There were apple trees, a peach tree, and a neglected raspberry patch, and behind the cottage a range of stone outbuildings, including a woodshed still stacked with dry logs. All it lacked was the greenhouse, and that was easily remedied.

Inside, she pottered around, visualizing the firelight winking on her few pieces of silver and the furniture she had garnered so carefully over the years. Up in the bedroom she admired the white walls and the sagging oak-beamed ceiling, and peered out of the tiny casement window below the thatch, gazing into the shadowy woods. "Chintz," she said. "I can go chintz mad."

"I beg your pardon," said the agent, an apprehensive young man in his early twenties.

Polly flushed. She had not realized that she had spoken aloud. She had even forgotten that the estate agent was with her. There and then she made up her mind. She would buy Summercombe Cottage, and as she came to her decision the years fell away, years of dusty, chalk-impregnated classrooms, with their hordes of unruly, shrieking children, years of marking papers, and endless academic argument in the smoke-laden atmosphere of shabby staff rooms. At last she was free, and there was no one in the world to dictate to her.

The agent was delighted, for none knew better than he the defects of Summercombe Cottage, isolated, drafty, and damp, and riddled with woodworm. Her solicitor thought her quite mad, and said so in no uncertain terms. "You are preparing to invest almost all your life savings into a property which needs considerable improvement and repair, a property which will prove almost unsalable if, after a few months there, you find you can't bear the loneliness. You really ought to reconsider, Miss Shaw."

But Polly was adamant. She sat in her chair, a plump, defiant little figure, her dark hair gathered in a bun at the nape of her neck, and her chin quivered with determination as she resisted all efforts to dissuade her. So it came about that in a remarkably short space of time, at dusk on an autumn day, she struck a match and lit the first fire in her new home. As the yellow flames licked hungrily at the dry sticks, the scent of wood smoke evoked memories of summers long ago, when she had been a captain of Girl Guides, and gangling girls now grown to be mothers with children of their own. She poured herself some coffee and sat down amid the packing cases and cartons that littered the floor, while outside the last light faded from the hills. There was no hurry to unpack. She had only herself to please, and there was all winter ahead. At least the cottage had electricity. On impulse she jumped from her chair and rushed around turning on all the lights. Then she went out into the garden.

The stars shone white in the cold air above the sheltering shoulders of the hills, and the dark and brooding trees seemed to crowd around the cottage and hold it out to her, a glowing casket of light, as if to say, "This is our most precious possession. Take it and cherish it."

Alone in the darkness, she felt the presence of the earth as a living, sentient being, and at that moment she felt more at one with the valley and the hills and the silent trees than she did with her fellow men. It was a feeling that was to grow, in the weeks that followed, as by day she labored in the garden, and by night sat at her sewing machine, or wielded a paintbrush in the darker, more cobwebby corners of the cottage.

One of her first acts was to hang a bird table from the bough of the damson tree. She found an old slab of elm wood, nearly two inches thick, and screwed hooks into each of the four corners. Then she hung chains from the bough of the tree and hooked the slab to them, carefully adjusting the height until the table was level. From the table she hung hoppers for peanuts and sunflower seeds, lumps of fat and suet, a large marrow bone, and pieces of bacon rind. Her first task each morning was to replenish the table, and then she could sit and enjoy her own breakfast, as the birds arrived to take theirs.

She was astonished at the variety of the visitors. Blackbirds and thrushes hopped about on the grass beneath the tree. Chaffinches and greenfinches, hedge sparrows and linnets jostled and pushed each other on the table, and were themselves chivied by a solitary robin. Tits came: blue tits, great tits, a cole tit, and a pair of willow tits, in such a confusion of color and design that Polly had to buy a bird book in order to identify them all. Nuthatches were regular visitors, and occasionally a woodpecker arrived, his vermilion cap nodding as he surveyed what was on offer.

Polly was also amazed at the amount of food consumed. Whoever coined the phrase "an appetite like a bird's," has never met this lot, she thought, as she prepared yet another bowl of scraps.

Late one evening she sat beside the window. The curtains remained undrawn, and the window was open, for the weather had remained dry, and the nights unseasonably warm. A book lay on her lap. She sat thinking over what she had just read, for one of her self-imposed tasks on retirement was a study of comparative religions. In recent years she had found herself increasingly at odds with the simple faith in which she had been raised, and which she had taught to generations of children. Now she wondered if the fault lay in herself or in the creed by which she had tried to live, and she was determined to find out. Already she had discovered the immensity of her task, but she persevered, hoping the work would get easier as she progressed.

A muffled squeaking in the garden roused her from her reveries, and she peered cautiously out of the window, hardly daring to breathe lest she frightened whatever it was away. Out of the shadows, and into the pool of light beneath the damson tree, came a family of hedgehogs, looking like animated pincushions as they waddled across the turf on short, bandy legs. They fell upon the remains of the bird food on the lawn with squeals of delight, and foraged busily around, moving surprisingly fast for such ungainly-looking creatures.

Polly watched entranced, until finally they trundled off into the night. Later she lay in bed wondering what she could do to encourage them to stay. Hedgehogs, she had read somewhere, were most beneficial to gardeners, eating all manner of insect pests. Even if they weren't, she thought, they were worth fostering for their entertainment value. She had to go into town the following day, so she would see what she could find.

The town was hot and noisy and smelly after the peace of Summercombe wood, and the people seemed more surly and ill mannered than ever. Polly was glad when she could load her week's provisions into the back of her old Morris, and drive back up into the valley. At the farm she stopped to collect her milk, and to ask if, for the next few days at least, she could have an extra pint.

"Expecting company then, Miss Shaw?" Mrs. Fletcher's curiosity about her nearest heighbor did not get enough nourishment to satisfy it.

"Why, no," began Polly, and then hesitated. She had been about to say she wanted to put a bowl of milk out for some hedgehogs, and then decided not to. She was considered eccentric enough in the village without giving cause for further gossip. "I, I get very thirsty working in the garden, and milk is very nourishing."

Fattening too, thought Mrs. Fletcher, eyeing Polly's plump, rounded figure with a certain amount of envy. She was as thin as a beanpole, as her husband was tactless enough to remind her. Aloud she said, "You can take an extra pint now if you wish."

Polly accepted gladly, and hastened away before the farmer's wife could question her further. Ridiculous, she thought, a woman of my age afraid of answering a straight question, guilty of a silly lie. I must be turning into a recluse.

Yet her sense of relief when she reached the sanctuary of her cottage was almost overwhelming, and it worried her.

"What comes of being alone too much, I suppose," she murmured to herself. "Now I'm even talking to myself. Perhaps I ought to invite a friend or two for the odd weekend?" Even as the thought phrased itself, she knew the idea had no appeal.

She dumped the carton of groceries on the kitchen floor, and rummaged around until she found the packet of cat food she had bought. It was a garishly colored package with a picture of a fat, complacent cat licking its lips. Polly read the instructions carefully. FIT KIT came in five different flavors, liver, fish, beef, chicken, and rabbit. It was a complete cat food, containing all necessary proteins, carbohydrates and fats, minerals, vitamins, and trace elements, and could be fed wet or dry. Polly opened the packet. Rather cleverly, she thought, she had chosen the rabbit flavor.

It looked revolting. She emptied the food into two bowls, poured the extra pint of milk over them, and then carried them out into the garden, setting them down under the damson tree. Then she returned to the house, to prepare something that looked a little more appetizing for herself, before assuming her vigil beside the window.

They came soon after dark, having remembered from the previous night that there were some very interesting tidbits to be found beneath the tree. It occurred to Polly that she had been overgenerous with the cat food, but even so she was astounded at the amount the hedgehogs were able to consume. They ate and ate, but it was not mere gluttony that drove them to excess. Soon the frosts would come, and the bitter winds of winter, and when that time came the hedgehogs would seek some refuge that was sheltered and dry. There, buried beneath dried grass and leaves, they would fall asleep. Their body temperature would fall, their heartbeats slow, and their breathing almost cease, as they sank deeper and deeper into a coma that would last until the warm days of spring.

In readiness for that time, the hedgehogs were now accumulating a thick layer of fat, enough fuel to drive the fires of life, to keep their metabolic processes just ticking through the long winter months. The young hedgehogs in particular had to reach a certain body weight if they were to survive. So through September and October they ate and ate and ate.

Even so, they did not quite manage to empty the bowls before they moved off, and Polly left the remains of the food on the lawn, in case the hedgehogs returned later in the night. She went to bed feeing very pleased with the success of her experiment, and fell asleep wondering if the manufacturers of FIT KIT ever imagined that their product would be used for feeding hedgehogs. Her last conscious thought was a fervent hope that it would not upset their stomachs.

At that moment, Borun and Vandal entered the garden.

9. The Intruders

For both animals, the task of finding food had of late grown more difficult. The rabbits had virtually ceased to breed for the season, and those litters that had survived the first few weeks of existence had grown lean and fast and wary. The prolonged drought had not helped. The earthworms had hidden themselves away until the coming of the rains, and the ground was baked harder than stone. Worse, for Borun, was the fact that the acorn crop had failed, and so instead of being able to stuff himself on the hard, bitter fruit, he had to be content with the few that the wood pigeons missed.

Like the hedgehogs, Borun needed at this time to accumulate a layer of fat, against the time of the hard weather, when instead of foraging he would pass the long nights drowsing in the warmth and security of the set. For Vandal the problem was not so serious, although normally he would have put on some weight at this time of year. Both he and Borun, moreover, were still growing, and the demands of muscle and bone had to be met. Though far from starving, their appetites were keen, and so they had taken to roving farther afield. On this night, greatly daring, they had come to explore the garden of the cottage.

They found the food the hedgehogs had left almost immediately, and Vandal, who had not tasted cat food or milk for a long while, soon cleared one bowl. Borun, slightly more suspicious, sniffed the food carefully, but after a few tentative licks he found it to his liking. He polished the bowl, turned it over in the hope of finding more underneath, and then, disappointed, began scavenging under the damson tree for the scraps that had fallen from the bird table.

The taste of the cat food revived old memories for Vandal, and Borun looked up from his foraging to see the cat sneaking away round the corner of the house. Borun followed, to find Vandal sniffing at the back door.

The cat-flap was still there. Vandal pushed cautiously, and it opened. He stood for a moment, his head just inside the kitchen, listening and waiting in case anything stirred. All was still, and he slid through into the house, the flap closing behind him. After a second's hesitation, Borun followed him, and for a long time the pair stood motionless, eager to explore further, yet poised for instant flight.

Polly had never been a tidy housekeeper, and since she had come to live alone she had grown more and more heedless of convention. The groceries she had bought that day still stood in their carton on the kitchen floor, and Borun, ever curious, was eager to discover what treasure this strange square tree stump might contain.

It came apart easily enough, and Borun's strong claws were soon ripping through cardboard and paper and plastic.

A flour bag broke first, but after a few licks Borun turned his attention elsewhere. Cornflakes were much nicer. Borun crunched happily for a while, until he found the sugar. This was better than all the wasps' nests in Somerset, and Borun licked and scrunched, all the time burrowing deeper into the carton.

Vandal watched disinterestedly, even when Borun unearthed another packet of FIT KIT. What Vandal craved was a long cool drink of milk. He remembered that in the past, all he had had to do was to rub himself against the door of the refrigerator and mew, and his mistress would open the door, take out the milk, and pour it into a bowl. Automatically, Vandal went through the routine, not once, but several times.

Nothing happened. No one came, and Borun was still head and shoulders inside the carton, oblivious to everything but the sugar. Indeed, he might have stayed there all night, had he not broken into a packet of detergent. He came out backward as if he had been shot from a gun, snorting and sneezing. When he had recovered somewhat he saw Vandal scratching and rubbing against the refrigerator door.

Unfortunately for Polly, the door of the refrigerator was of the kind that is held by a magnetic catch, and it presented no problem to Borun. Three rashers of bacon, some cheese, and an egg disappeared inside the badger, while Vandal pushed and mewed, still impatient for his milk.

It stood on a shelf in a jug. As Borun stood up on his hindlegs and thrust his greedy little snout further into the refrigerator he dislodged the shelf. The jug slid forward, and Vandal got his milk, rather more than he required, all over his head and shoulders.

The crash of the falling jug woke Polly. She lay for a moment, cold fear clutching her heart. Then she pulled herself together, and got out of bed. If there were intruders in the house, it was better she faced them standing, than abed at their mercy. With any luck, they would not realize she was alone in the house, and if she gave them plenty of warning, they might flee.

Noisily she opened the bedroom door, stood for a moment on the landing, and then began to clump heavily downstairs. Outside the living room she stopped and listened, but no sound except the ticking of the clock came to her ears, so at last, screwing up all her courage, she stepped inside and turned on the light.

All seemed to be in order. Her handbag was just where she had left it on the table, and the silver candlesticks were on the mantelpiece as usual. Perhaps it had all been a dream. By now, however, she was thoroughly awake, and she decided to make a hot drink to take back to bed.

Her first reaction when she saw the kitchen was one of horror and disgust. The shambles that was once a cardboard carton held a revolting mixture of flour, sugar, cornflakes, and cat food, all mixed with detergent. The floor was strewn with torn scraps of paper and cardboard, and covered with floury footprints. The refrigerator door was open, its contents warming in a pool of milk.

Then Polly spotted the milky paw marks leading to the cat-flap, and she realized what must have happened, although she was unsure about the exact identity of her nocturnal visitors. It wasn't hedgehogs, she was sure, and while some of the prints looked like those of a cat, others were larger. Certainly no cat could wreak such havoc as this, yet whatever it was had to be small enough to get through the flap. Suddenly a mental image of Mrs. Fletcher came to her. "Expecting company then, Miss Shaw?" Standing there in the ruins of her kitchen, she began to laugh.

She went back upstairs and dressed, then set to work to clean up the kitchen. Ruefully she reflected that she would have to make another journey to town to replace those provisions that had been ruined, but first of all she meant to catch up on a few hours' lost sleep. Her last act before retiring was to nail a stout batten of wood across the cat-flap, and so prevent any further nocturnal visitations.

It was close on noon when next she woke, and consequently bedtime found her wide awake. Once again she had put out food for the hedgehogs, and they had been and gone. Still she sat on, hoping to discover the identity of the invaders of the previous night. She waited in vain. The moon rose and journeyed across the sky, the fire died in the hearth, and the room fell chill. At last, stiff and weary, she went to bed. Her sleep was undisturbed.

Vandal in fact had hunted alone that night, for Borun was feeling distinctly unwell, and reluctant to leave the set. By dusk of the following day, however, Borun had recovered from the effects of his overeating, and was once again eager for food. Together the pair set off, by tacit consent heading for the cottage, in hopes of finding more food under the damson tree.

The rattling of the bowls alerted Polly, and she peeped cautiously out the window. She saw Vandal at once, and at first thought he must have come up the track from the farm. Then she remembered Mrs. Fletcher telling her about a white kitten that was missing after the previous owner of the cottage had died, and wondered if it could be the same one that was now feeding on the lawn.

Borun had his back to the window, and at first she did not notice his gray form. Then suddenly he turned, and Polly caught her breath in surprise and delight. As she watched, Vandal disappeared around the side of the house, and she heard the rattle of the cat-flap. Suddenly, all was explained, and Polly now knew who the miscreant was who had all but wrecked her kitchen.

Vandal's attempts to gain entry to the kitchen failed, and he rejoined Borun on the lawn. Only when they were quite certain that not a single crumb of food remained uneaten did the pair move off into the night, leaving Polly alone at the window.

They came every night after that, and Polly made sure that there were adequate supplies of food available. On the third night she put the food out as usual, and then, dressed in warm dark clothing, she sat down at the foot of the damson tree.

Half an hour passed, and then she saw the white figure of the cat materialize out of the darkness. Close behind him came the young badger, and both animals made straight for the feeding bowls on the grass. Then Vandal noticed her and froze, one paw raised, ready to flee at the slightest sign of danger, but reluctant to forgo his supper unless it was absolutely necessary.

Polly sat motionless, hardly daring to breathe, and at long last Vandal relaxed, crept forward, and began to feed. Reassured, Borun did likewise, and found that as well as the usual cat food and milk, there was a slice of bread and honey in his bowl. This find went a long way toward easing his nervousness, and he cleared his plate before helping Vandal to finish his meal.

Each night Polly positioned the bowls a little closer to her, and within a week the pair were feeding beside her feet. Soon they were taking scraps from her hand, though both shied away if she tried to touch them. It did not occur to her to question the wisdom of her actions. She was merely amusing herself, and gave no thought to the fact that she might be endangering the young badger's chances of survival by making it dependent on her for food.

She was almost tempted to open up the cat-flap, but reluctantly she decided against it, for she saw very clearly that there was no way of making her kitchen badger proof, and the thought of the pair romping around her house at night convinced her that her plan was not practical.

So the nightly visits continued, as winter drew nearer and darkness came earlier each evening. Polly no longer sat under the damson tree to await her guests, but simply took the bowls out to them when they arrived. The nights were now cold, and frequently it was raining. For Polly, the novelty of the situation had worn off, and the arrival of her visitors merely necessitated one more chore.

Then, one night, Borun disgraced himself. Inevitably, sooner or later, the hedgehogs were bound still to be feeding when Borun and Vandal appeared. Polly had thought about this, but knowing the hedgehogs' trick of rolling into a tight prickly ball when molested, she felt quite sure that they would be safe. She did not know that badgers have a way of dealing with hedgehogs.

So, when the encounter finally did occur, Polly watched unconcerned, and with a certain amount of detached amusement. Three of the hedgehogs scattered and ran, but the fourth, which had delayed flight a little too long, curled into a ball. Borun strolled over to it. Gingerly, he rolled it on to its back, and then, before Polly could do anything to stop him, he plunged his claws deep into the place where the head of the hedgehog met its tail, and pried the unfortunate beast open. He gave one quick bite, the hedgehog squealed and died, and Borun was already crunching its skull when Polly attacked him with a broom.

Borun gave a gruff bark of fear and fled, closely followed by Vandal, leaving Polly to mourn the death of the hedgehog, and reflect rather shakily on the strength of the dark forces she had been impertinent enough to try and tame.

There was no supper for anyone the next night, but it did not matter, for nobody came. The hedgehogs were too afraid of meeting the badger again, and Borun was understandably reluctant to face an angry woman armed with a broom. Next morning, however, Vandal surprised Polly by appearing in broad daylight sitting on the garden wall and watching her with yellow eyes. She brought him a bowl of milk and he lapped it, before disappearing back into the woods.

He appeared more frequently after that, often hanging around the garden for hours at a time, and then, one night, as a gale roared through the trees and howled in the chimney, he scratched at the door. When Polly opened it he came in, to sit on the rug in front of the fire, as if he had never been away.

The explanation was quite simple. Borun was spending more and more time asleep in the set, and as winter wore on, life in the woods was growing ever more uncomfortable for Vandal. No longer could he pass the long day snoozing in the sun, and the dark, stuffy confines of the set were not particularly agreeable to him. So he had returned from the wild, and though he still saw Borun from time to time, they were no longer such close companions. The partnership, such as it was, had served its purpose, and now it was ended.

At first Polly was inclined to regard her adoption by Vandal with amused indignation, but then she remembered that recently she had suffered a minor invasion of fieldmice, also seeking shelter from the weather. On two occasions she had been forced to set traps in the kitchen, and each time she had sat in an agony of suspense, waiting for the "snap" that announced the execution of the furry little trespasser. Then she had had to face the distasteful business of disposing of the corpse.

Vandal, she knew, would relieve her of both tasks, and his presence in the cottage might deter further invaders. So he stayed, readily accepting a bowl of milk when it was offered, and occasionally a dish of cat food, though on the whole he preferred to hunt and catch his own food. Fortunately, he was disinterested in the birds that came to the bird table, or he might soon have disgraced himself in Polly's eyes. Instead, she came to look forward to his company during the long winter evenings, and the soothing sound of his deep-throated purr, as he relaxed by the fire.

10. One Eye

One Eye the vixen came to Summercombe in the new year, when the January moon shone white over a valley bare of snow, but locked in the grip of a hard black frost. Here she was courted and won by the old dog fox that lived at the top of the wood, and for a fortnight the woods and hillsides echoed to the sound of their love calls. Each evening the vixen's scream, loud and haunting, told her need and desire, and always in answer came the triple bark of the dog fox. Ever and again the calls were repeated, until at last the two came together, to be united under the stars.

The courtship was torrid, but brief, and afterward the pair went their separate ways, the dog fox back to his old haunt in the wood, and the vixen to the shelter of a gorse thicket high on the hill. Here she slept by day, basking in the pale winter sunlight, or lying curled in a ball, her pads tucked close to her body, and her face and nose covered by the dense brush of her tail. Thus protected, she was impervious to the cold.

By night she hunted, leaving the shelter of the gorse thicket each dusk to stalk the rabbits that had already begun to breed again among the hedgerows, or to wait patiently beside a ditch, watching and listening for the telltale rustle and the bright dark eye of an emerging vole. She was quicker and more light-footed than a cat, and possessed of a cunning and patience that more than compensated for the loss of her eye.

It was now almost a year since the injury had occurred, late one afternoon when the world lay blanketed in deep snow. She had succeeded in stalking a heron, that wiliest of birds, as it stood in the shallow waters of a stream that flowed sluggishly between ice-rimmed banks.

As she sprang, the vixen's hindfoot slipped on the ice, and although she seized her prey, it was by the wing rather than the throat. In the struggle that followed, in a flurry of icy spray, the daggerlike beak of the heron caught her across the eye. A moment later the heron died, as the vixen's teeth closed on her throat, and in her savage joy the killer barely noticed her own injury. She ate as much of the heron as she could manage, and then buried the remains in a snowdrift, leaving one scaly foot exposed, as if in a last silent tribute to a world that had betrayed it. It was later found by a buzzard, who had not fed for three days, and would have died if it had spent one more night with an empty crop.

The vixen's injury seemed trifling, but gradually the scratched cornea turned opaque and white, leaving her blind on one side. In the weeks that followed, One Eye fared badly, as she learned to adjust to her impediment. Consequently she did not breed that year, and the unborn cubs she now carried in her womb were to be her first litter. So the days passed, and as the icy bonds of winter melted before the warm breath of spring, One Eye's flanks grew a little rounder and thicker, but if she was perhaps a little slower on her feet, it still meant no reprieve for the rabbits of Summercombe.

On a bright day in late March, as the daffodils in the churchyard shone yellow amid the gray of the headstones, and the sable rooks in the elms above solemnly discussed the mechanics of repairing their nests, a cheerful assembly gathered on the village green. Riders on horseback clattered in from all directions, some resplendent in hunting scarlet, others wearing nondescript habits and jodhpurs. Ruddy-faced farmers in weather-worn tweeds sat astride heavy hunters, and sallow-cheeked children nervously straddled fat ponies, each silently praying that he or she would not disgrace themselves by inadvertently breaking the unwritten but complex code of the hunting field. The master sat a little to one side, raising his hunting crop in salute to each newcomer, and talking quietly to his groom, all the while keeping one eye on the church clock.

The landlord of the village inn bustled about, chivying his wife and daughters, who bore trays laden with glasses of amber liquid, as they handed round the traditional stirrup cup. The rest of the villagers looked on, enjoying the spectacle of the North Somerset Foxhounds gathering in Summercombe. The church clock struck eleven, and the hounds moved off, flowing in a liver and white stream up the lane that led to Bidewell Farm. With a creaking of leather and jingling of harness the horses followed, while those who were to follow the hunt by foot or by car also moved away, each to seek the best vantage point for watching the chase. In a few moments the square was deserted, except for the landlord of the inn, and the bent, stooping figure of Bill Fernybrass. Bill was a fanatical gardener, and winner of all the prizes at the annual village flower show. Now he was reaping, with bucket and shovel, an eagerly awaited harvest of horse manure to spread beneath his roses.

One Eye, asleep in the gorse thicket, heard the clamor of the hounds as they poured through the valley, and watched as they spread out over the hillside opposite, to converge on a small clump of hawthorn bushes, that stood stark, black, and leafless amid a sea of rust-red bracken. After a few minutes they moved on, drawing each small corpse and thicket in turn, and gradually working their way along the hillside until they reached the head of the valley. Here they turned about, and made their way back toward the farm, following the floor of the valley, threading in and out of the hedges and ditches and checking every bramble patch and weed-strewed ruin. Finally, they turned about again, to cover the hill where One Eye lay.

Even then One Eye did not move, until, rising and falling on the breeze, she heard the clamor of the hounds' tongues as they sang their death song. Then she slipped away, climbing the hill until she reached the rocky ramparts of the old hill fort. Here, among the gray limestone rocks and the stunted, twisted thorn trees, she rested, waiting as the hounds found her scent in the gorse thicket, and followed the running line of her flight.

As the hounds crested the hill she moved again, and the russet gleam of her coat was spotted by a watcher standing on the site of the old fort. The man waved his hat and yelled to the hunt, who toiled behind the hounds on mud-spattered horses, and spurs dug into flanks as the riders urged their mounts forward. Hounds fanned out, foaming through the rocks and withered fern, and then came a renewal of their song as they converged once more upon her scent.

She led them downhill now, back into the valley and up toward its head. Twice she lost them, once when she dived into a drain which led through a hedge mound, and through which hounds could not follow. Here she gained some time, as hounds bayed in frustration at the entrance to the drain, until an older, wiser hound mounted the hedge bank and picked up her scent on the other side.

One Eye, crouched panting in a ditch, heard the music of the hounds ring out above the pounding of her heart, and ran once more. For a second time she managed to throw them off the scent, by zigzagging to and fro between the terrified members of a flock of sheep, and again she managed to snatch a few moments of much needed rest, before she was on her feet once more.

She was slower now. Her tongue lolled, and her one good eye was glazed as she gained the shelter of the wood, and the panting of her labored breath was clearly audible as she stood beneath the sheltering trees, listening again for the sounds of pursuit. Still the hounds came on, and she circled around, keeping just inside the wood, but following the hedge that divided the trees from the field. Just before she reached the highest point of the woodlands, she passed within a few feet of the old dog fox.

Now her strength was failing fast. She staggered as she ran, and once she fell, to lie on her side for a brief moment before plunging on. She wanted to regain the sanctuary of the fort, to try and lose the hounds among the welter of boulders and weather-worn limestone that littered the crown of the hill, but she knew she was not equal to the task. Instead, she turned downhill, following the worn badger track that wound through the undergrowth.

She reached the entrance to the badger set, and for a moment she paused, and in that instant of time she realized that the hounds were no longer following her, that the hideous belling cry that had haunted her throughout the afternoon was gradually growing fainter. It mattered little. She could run no further, and here was sanctuary of a sort. Gratefully, she slipped into the tunnel, and when she found a chamber, lined with old and musty bedding, she collapsed.

Ten minutes later and a mile away, after a screaming run that led hounds in a dead straight line across country, that left the horses far behind and unseated two riders, the old dog fox was torn to pieces by the hounds. It mattered nothing to him.

His old heart had burst, seconds before, and he was dead long before the first hound closed on him. He won fame, of a kind, in the annals of the hunt, as an old warrior who had provided one of the longest runs of the century. Only the whipper-in guessed the truth, and perhaps the master, but one was too cautious, and the other too wise, to spoil the beginnings of a legend.

11. The Squatters

Borun was not immediately aware of the presence of his uninvited guest. The refuge One Eye had chosen was the old nursery, a part of the set Borun rarely visited, and so it was not until dusk fell that the badger, emerging, found the atmosphere around the set redolent with the musky odor of fox. He tracked the scent to its source, and having confirmed his suspicions that he now had a new neighbor, he departed on the night's forage, grumbling to himself as he trotted down the track. There was nothing he could do about the situation, even if it had occurred to him to take action, which it did not. To the badger, foxes—like frost, and snow, and ache in the bones—were an inevitable fact of life.

For sixteen hours One Eye lay exhausted in the nursery

set. Then, as the gray dawn turned to silver over the misty landscape, she crawled from the set and made her way stiffly through the wood in search of water. She found it at the limestone spring, and having drunk her fill, limped painfully back to the set. Here she met Borun, and the two animals stared in hostility at each other before disappearing into their separate quarters. Time, and destiny, had caught up with One Eye, and now she could not leave the set, even if she had wanted to.

In the next four hours she gave birth to four cubs, all naked, blind, and helpless. In spite of the mental trauma their mother had suffered, and her physical ordeal of the previous day, the cubs were strong and lusty, and they all thrived. Within fourteen days their eyes were open, and at three weeks they made their first stumbling appearance at the mouth of the set, small, sooty, furred imps with bright eyes, short pointed noses, and big ears, wobbling about on rubbery legs and waving ridiculous little wisps of tails.

For a week or so the cubs played at the mouth of the set, romping like kittens under the watchful eye of their mother, and when Borun passed they sat very still and upright, affording Borun the respect a child might have for an elderly and crochety uncle. Then, as the cubs grew older, their mother began to wean them.

The woods and fields of the valley were alive with young birds and animals too silly and inexperienced to survive for long, and One Eye brought back to the set young rabbits and pheasant chicks, voles, mice and leverets, lapwing, partridge, and moorhen. Occasionally she even brought lizards and slow worms, and once a luckless green woodpecker, caught napping as he probed the turf of the woodland floor for grubs late one evening. Mice and voles she brought by the mouthful, appearing at the set with the tiny corpses packed sideways between her jaws, the tails hanging down on either side of her nuzzle like a drooping walrus moustache.

After a while she began to bring back her victims maimed, but not dead, and these she released for the cubs to chase and kill. She brought back more, far more, than either she or the cubs could eat. Gradually the arena around the set became littered with the remains of small corpses, many of which the cubs continued to use as playthings, the pelt of a rabbit, the wing of a moorhen, the leg and foot of a pheasant.

Now the sweet sickly scent of rotting flesh was added to the aroma of fox, and during the warm sunny days the air was loud with the buzzing of blowflies, come to lay their eggs on the rotting meat. Some of the flies even found their way into Borun's sleeping quarters, and roused him from his slumber. It was getting to be too much for him to bear.

The climax came one night in early June. For some days One Eye had realized that conditions in the nursery set were growing too cramped for herself and four lumping great cubs. The air was hot and stuffy, and what remained of the bedding was foul and verminous. A move was imperative, and so, taking advantage of Borun's absence, One Eye went on an exploration of the main set. She found Borun's sleeping chamber, freshly lined with grass and dry leaves, and knew at once that nothing could suit her needs better. Just before dawn she led her cubs down there, the last and smallest cub bringing up the rear and dragging his favorite plaything, the rabbit pelt, behind him. This he abandoned three feet inside the entrance to the tunnel.

Borun returned to find his entrance defiled and putrid with the stench of fox, and he did not need the evidence of the rabbit skin to tell him what had happened. One by one he inspected every entrance to the set, and in each case his nose told him the same story, that the entire set was contaminated by the presence of the foxes. It was too much. He could not endure the discomfort and the mess any longer. Abruptly he turned away from the set and padded off into the wood. For a moment his humped gray back was visible among the undergrowth, and then he was lost in the shadows of the trees.

He took the path uphill, and as the sun crested the horizon he entered the tangle of rock and twisted thorn that clung like old gray chain mail to the hillside below the Iron Age fort. Here he spent the day, curled in a tight ball at the foot of a gnarled old hawthorn tree, and apart from the steady rise and fall of his breathing, he was indistinguishable from the stones and boulders that littered the hill.

The shade of the tree had sheltered him from the heat of the noonday sun, but now its westering rays struck warm upon his flank, waking him and bringing him to remembrance of where he was. For a while he lay basking in the warmth and light, but as the sun sank below the shoulder of the hill he got up, scratched, and shook himself before setting off into what was for him unexplored territory.

He crossed the windswept plateau of the old fort, picking up an occasional beetle from the short, sheep-bitten turf, but all the while heading purposefully southeast, away from the valley of his birth. Soon he was in farmland again, wide fields planted with barley and root crops, and surrounded by carefully tended hedges and banks. A barn owl, drifting white and ghostlike over the land, swerved in startled surprise as Borun raised his black and white snout skyward, and a hunting stoat chattered angrily from the safety of the tangled hedge roots as he passed by.

Then he came to woodland again, a plantation of young spruce trees growing tall above the rotting stumps of what had once been giant old oaks, trees that had been felled so that the swifter-growing conifers could provide a cash crop for the farmer. Borun tried in vain to find a way into the plantation, but the area had been well and truly fenced off by the farmer, who was only too familiar with the sort of damage that rabbits and roe deer would cause once they gained entry. So Borun skirted around the plantation until he came to older, deciduous woodland, with a narrow rutted track, twisting between high banks, and still littered with the leaves of the previous autumn.

On top of the bank tall beech trees grew, their trunks silver in the moon that now shone down out of a starlit sky. Their tough old roots twisted and twined like great gray serpents over the eroded remains of the bank, while overhead the branches met in a graceful arc to form a canopy of leaves, black and metallic in the lunar light. The trees had stood there, season after season, surviving winter gales and summer drought, hail and rain and biting frost. They were at once a monument and a reminder that perhaps our forefathers were better conservationists than we give them credit for.

Some two hundred years ago a farsighted landowner had planted these beech trees, along with thousands of others, as part of a new and revolutionary system of farming known as a four-crop rotation. To this end he had divided his land into fields, surrounding each one with a hedge and a ditch, and the saplings he chose for his hedges were all beech. Once the saplings had taken firm root, the hedges were "laid." The saplings were cut halfway through, and laid over one against the other, and pegged down. The saplings did not die, but put forth fresh green growth, so that in a very short time they formed a stockproof barrier, and since the dead leaves hung on through the winter, they provided shelter from wind and rain.

At the same time, by allowing sections of hedge to sprout up, the farmer assured himself of a constant supply of firewood, that came in handy ten-foot lengths, and was exactly the right thickness for easy cutting and burning. After the firewood had been harvested, the fence was once more laid, and the cycle began anew.

Then came the industrial revolution, and a cheap and

seemingly inexhaustible supply of coal. Following that came a world war, and a shortage of manpower coincided with the invention of barbed wire, so that the beech hedgerow became an expensive anachronism. Except in a few districts, it disappeared from the country scene. Here, all that remained of the hedge was a twin avenue of tall trees, which for almost a century had escaped the power saw and the ax.

Rabbits swarmed among the beech roots, secure behind a tangled trelliswork that defied Borun's attempts to dig them out, but the deep litter of leafmold that lay in the track provided rich pickings in the way of worms and grubs. Borun dug and grunted happily, working his slow way down the track as the moon sailed her course across the sky.

As the short summer night came to an end, and the thin line of dawn brightened the northeastern sky, Borun came to a hole in the earth bank. It was little more than an overgrown rabbit burrow, scratched and dug and tunneled by generations of rabbits, but there was ample room for Borun, and he clambered inside. After a short distance underground, the tunnel widened out into a sizable chamber beneath a beech bole, and here Borun surprised a startled doe rabbit, who was too witless to flee. Borun grabbed her, and twenty minutes later, feeling uncomfortably full, settled to sleep.

Some hours later he awoke to instant alertness, roused by the deep-throated barking of a dog. He lay still, listening, and then came a scratching at the mouth of the tunnel, not three feet away. There came another bark, and then an excited, high-pitched whining, followed by a soft, snuffling sound. Suddenly the chamber was filled with the scent of dog, and Borun backed against the far wall, head down, hair bristling, and white teeth bared, ready to fight to the death if need be. Next moment he relaxed, as the dog suddenly moved away.

Outside in the lane the black Labrador raced after his master, in obedience to the gamekeeper's whistle. The man growled at him affectionately, "Who gave you leave to go off rabbiting, I'd like to know? Come in to heel."

Obediently the dog fell in behind the man, who walked on, his gun crooked comfortably over his arm. Again he spoke, more to himself than to the dog. "I see the pheasants have been feeding well in the lane. There's fresh leaves upturned that weren't disturbed yesterday."

12. The River

Borun passed an uneasy day in the hole under the beech tree. Long before sunset he was waiting at the mouth of the hole, anxious to be away from this place with its threat of danger from man and dog. He was in fact doubly fortunate, in that the retriever had warned him of his peril so soon after his arrival on the estate, and that the gamekeeper had so far failed to notice his presence. For Borun had unwittingly strayed onto a game preserve. The old deciduous woodland had been allowed to remain merely to act as cover for the pheasants that swarmed in the undergrowth.

In the autumn many of these birds would die, shot by syndicates of businessmen who were prepared to pay high fees for the privilege of hunting them, and so the pheasants represented a cash crop to the farmer, as valuable in its way as the cereals and root crops he grew. In consequence the woodlands were managed as efficiently as the rest of the farm. Borun's presence would not have gone unnoticed for long, and it would not have been tolerated, even though it posed little threat to the pheasant population.

The pheasants were flying to roost as Borun left his hideout, exploding out of the undergrowth with a clatter of wings and perching in the branches of the trees, their plump forms dark silhouettes against the night sky. Borun passed beneath them, following the course of a grassy ride that traversed the woodland, and soon he was out in open country again, crossing wide flat fertile fields which ended abruptly in an escarpment of low limestone cliffs. Below the cliffs a belt of thick woodland fell away to more open parkland, with tall trees casting deep pools of shadow in the bright moonlight. Beyond the park, shimmering like a silver snake, lay the broad sweep of the river.

The river was old and wide, meandering through fields and meadows, loitering on the last stage of its journey to the sea. A major artery of the land, it was fed by scores of tributaries, pouring their waters down out of the hills that lay to the east and south. Though cold and infertile at first, these waters contained one priceless asset, for they welled up out of the chalk, and they were rich in dissolved calcium.

Slowed down and sun warmed, the river maintained an immeasurable quantity and diversity of life, as the calcium provided a rich, alkaline medium in which vegetable and animal plankton flourished. This in turn supported vast armies of freshwater shrimps and insects, which contributed to the great size of the fish, the chub and trout, the perch and pike and roach. Eventually the calcium found its way to the teeth and bones of the water voles and otters, and to the eggshells of the coot and moorhen and mallard that nested on the banks. So a legacy laid down millions of years ago was returned once more to the living, for the chalk was formed out of the skeletons of other creatures, now long extinct, which once had swarmed in the sunlit shallow waters of a tropical sea.

Each winter, when the rains came, the volume of water cascading down out of the hills was too much for the river to carry away to the sea, and at least once or twice every year the river broke its banks, spreading its waters, laden with a heavy burden of silt, over the meadows on either side. This flooding enriched the pastures, and the grass grew lush and thick as the waters subsided in the spring, in turn supporting a wealth of life. Moles busily pursued the earthworms in the soft soil. Voles and mice squeaked and scurried through the grass roots, and in turn were harried by weasels and owls.

So Borun fed well that night, and the next, hiding by day in the dark recesses of a huge old hollow oak tree that had fallen one night in a winter gale ten years previously, and now lay in a corner of a field, conveniently out of the farmer's way, and overgrown with a thick tangle of bramble and briar rose.

He woke, late on the evening of the second day, to a strange hubbub and disturbance. Footsteps reverberated along the riverbank. Men called to each other on the still evening air. Somewhere in the distance, car doors were slamming. A transistor radio played tinny music, and a paraffin stove hissed as its flames blossomed like a blue rose around the base of a kettle.

Nervously, Borun peered out from the curtain of foliage that sheltered the entrance to his hideaway, unable to comprehend the sight that met his eyes. As far as he could see in the rapidly gathering dusk, men lined the river on both banks. Others were still arriving, each laden down with a mountain of gear, and carrying a bundle of fishing rods, the latecomers tramping past those who had already arrived, in search of a vacant space by the river. Meantime, those who had earlier staked their claims were busy assembling their rods, and setting up a variety of other items, such as large umbrellas, collapsible chairs, and beds. Here and there, some were even erecting tents.

Borun was witnessing what had now become an annual event in modern England, the opening night of the coarse fishing season. Nobody quite knew how many anglers there were. Some estimated the figure at three million, but this included the more solitary anglers for salmon and trout, and those who fished in the sea. Yet the greater proportion of anglers were the so-called coarse fishermen, who fished for freshwater species other than salmon and trout, and who angled purely for sport, returning their catch to the river at the end of each outing. The association that leased the fishing rights of this river had its headquarters in a city some twenty miles away, and the membership of the association numbered over ten thousand. Not every member turned out on the opening night, but the fishermen arrived in sufficient numbers to have a massive impact on their surroundings.

Borun waited for more than three hours, but the fishermen showed no signs of moving, so he slipped out of the hollow tree and made his way upstream, giving the riverbank a wide berth. After a journey of a mile or so, he realized that the serried ranks of anglers had come to an end. He had crossed the boundary of that stretch of river that the association leased, and he was now on land where the riparian owner kept the fishing for himself. So for the remainder of the night he foraged successfully and in peace, and because no suitable resting place offered itself, he returned at dawn to the hollow tree, noting, as he crept quietly into the bramble thicket, that the anglers were still there.

Many of the anglers returned to the city later in the morning, to sleep, or to yawn their way through a weary day at office or factory. Next evening other anglers came to the riverbank to take their place, and so it would continue throughout the summer, with numbers dwindling as the earlier novelty wore off, but always with someone in attendance by day or night. The anglers caught many fish, and some died as a result of handling, but most survived and lived to grow larger, and be caught another day.

The anglers had a profound effect on the country scene. The sheer weight of their numbers eroded the banks, and wore the grass bare, killing it so that when the winter floods came the grass no longer held the banks in place, and the floodwaters washed them away.

Many anglers used bread in large quantities, not only to bait their hooks, but as ground bait, throwing it into the stream to attract shoals of fish to the area around their hooks. Often surplus bread was left lying on the bank, or was thrown into the rushes bordering the stream, and while much of it was eaten by birds, the remainder attracted rats, who took up permanent residence by the stream.

Most of the anglers were considerate and thoughtful, at pains to preserve the beauty of a landscape they valued almost as much as the fishing itself, but a few were careless and untidy, leaving litter, always unsightly, and often dangerous. Small rodents squeezed their way into discarded bottles, only to starve when they found themselves unable to climb out up the slippery sides. Birds were trapped, snared by lengths of nylon monofilament line, which cut into their legs so tightly that even if they did not die, the victims escaped only at the cost of losing a limb. The majority of anglers were quick to condemn such practices, however, and most were agreed that much as they enjoyed the camaraderie of the riverbank, they would be only too happy to exchange it for solitude, and a stretch of the river to themselves. As things were, the very popularity of their sport was going a long way to destroying it.

Borun soon noticed that the anglers kept strictly to the riverbank, and deciding that they posed no threat to him, he came and went pretty much as he pleased, always being careful, however, to keep a safe distance away, and to enter and leave his hideout with extreme caution. All the same, he was observed by one or two keen-eyed anglers, who regarded his appearance as an added bonus to the fishing expedition, and were careful to leave him unmolested.

The month dragged on in sullen heat, as the brassy glare of the sun parched the earth, baking the muddy margins of the river so that they grew cracked and hard. By night a warm wind blew, so that no dew fell to freshen the dusty pastures. In the fields, sweating farmhands labored to bring in the hay, and gazing skyward, foretold the coming of the storm.

It broke late one afternoon. All day thunder had been muttering in the far-off hills, causing the pheasants in the copses to crow as if in answer. Already the waterfowl on the river had moved deep into the reedbeds for safety, warned of impending disaster by the slight, almost imperceptible rise in the level of the river, and the gathering of tiny twigs and grasses, washed down from far upstream, which together with flecks of foam presaged the coming of the flood. As the day wore on the sky darkened from sulfur yellow to deepest bronze, and then to black, to a darkness so extreme that birds flew prematurely to roost.

Then came the wind, blowing strong and chill, turning the leaves of the alders so that they showed their silvery undersides, and as that died away the first lightning bolt rent the skies. Hail fell, stripping the leaves from the trees and pounding young and tender growth into a slimy green pulp. Insects died in their thousands, as did any small bird or mammal that had not heeded the warning signs, or had been unlucky in its choice of shelter. As the hail ceased, and torrential rain took its place, the lightning and the thunder became a continuous bedlam of light and sound. Far away, on the coast thirty miles to the west, the tide began to rise.

It was the time of the new moon, and far out in the ocean

the waters had responded to the combined pull of the sun and the moon. Now they were rushing back landward, flooding into the estuaries and inlets, just in time to meet the storm water thundering down off the hills, swelling the waters of the river, and finding no outlet.

There was only one way they could go, and as the rain continued to fall, the river rose, inch by slow inch, until the first trickles spilled out over the banks and sent creeping, questing fingers of muddy water out into the meadow. The trickles grew into streams, the streams became torrents, and at last a swelling brown tide, foam-flecked and strewn with flotsam, sticks, and branches, old tree stumps, bottles, plastic containers of every shape and hue and size, twigs, grasses, and fragments of leaves, wisps of hay, and the decayed empty husk of a newborn calf, which had been washed into the river during an earlier flood, and which had hung drying in the branches of a riverside tree ever since.

Borun woke to an unpleasant feeling of cold and wetness, and leapt up to find water flowing into the hollow log. Earlier he had heard the tumult of the storm, and had curled tighter into a ball, covering his ears with his paws to drown the din. Now he was to regret his heedlessness. Grumbling to himself, he waded out into the open. In the dim light he saw a brown sea spreading in every direction, and noticed a ripple of movement by his feet. A short-tailed vole was swimming in search of safety. When it reached the rough bark of the log it scrambled up, shook itself, and began to groom its fur. For a moment Borun was tempted to snap the vole up, but self-preservation came first. He set off, splashing through the flood, which came almost to the level of his chin, and making for higher ground.

Several times he was forced to swim. He passed more small rodents, more unfortunate even than the vole on the log, swimming aimlessly around in small circles that could only end, when cold and fear and exhaustion had done their work, in death. For the vole on the log, life was to be endured for another four hours, until a hunting owl spotted the small form and sank its talons deep in the vole's heart.

Borun was in no such danger, but he was cold and wet and thoroughly out of temper by the time he reached dry land. He shook himself vigorously, and groomed as much of the moisture as possible out of his coat, before setting out across the sodden landscape. He still followed the course of the river upstream, but gave the water meadows a wide berth. The river was rich, and offered an easy living, but it was also treacherous.

In the event, the storm was over, the rain ceased, the tide turned, and the floodwaters began to recede. With the dawn, a watery sun embraced a steaming world with its warmth, and from an ash tree in a wayside thicket a blackbird sang a hymn of praise and gratitude for survival. Deep in the thicket Borun grunted, and slept.

13. The Romanies

The thicket in which Borun had taken refuge was comprised of a few tall and stately ash trees, protected by a dense undergrowth of blackthorn. It stood in the middle of a patch of wasteland that lay at the meeting of two roads. Beyond the wasteland was a small wood, where clumps of hazel grew beneath old and pollarded oaks, and beyond that flowed a stream, its waters still swollen and brown from the rainfall of the previous night. A rough track led across the wasteland, following the boundary of the wood, and screened from the road by the thorn thicket. Coarse grasses covered the rest of the land, yellowing in the sun as their flowers turned to seed.

The long day dragged on in silence under the sun. Once a

magpie flew into the thicket, to perch on the topmost branch of the tallest tree, and his raucous cry, as he spotted Borun asleep in the shade, ripped the air like rifle fire. Then he flew away and was lost to sight beyond the wood. The wasteland was still again, save for the drone of countless insects, each busy with its own mysterious lifestyle. No one came near, for the roads, dusty and forgotten, belonged to a bygone age. The countryside, burdened with the ripening wheat, lay quietly awaiting the bustle and noise of the harvest.

The afternoon was almost over when the travelers arrived at the wasteland. They came driving slowly down the road, a motley cavalcade, and one by one pulled onto the track beside the wood, parking their vehicles behind the dense screen of the thorn thicket. First came an expensive saloon car, towing a large black and white caravan that sported lace curtains at the windows, and shone with trimmings of chromium plate. Next came an open truck, half loaded with a miscellaneous collection of junk, scrap metal, rags, and wooden crates, and also towing a caravan, which, though smaller, was just as opulent as the first. Finally came a closed van, towing a third caravan, older and cheaper than the others, but still shining with bright green paint and polish.

The travelers were Romanies, whose ancestors had migrated out of India centuries ago, to travel west and spread out across the whole of Europe and, in spite of persistent persecution, to survive. This family, the older man and his wife, the two sons and their wives, together with four children, a goat, a crate of hens, and a pack of lean, hungry mongrel dogs, had been strawberry picking down in the south and were now moving slowly north to Gloucester, where soon there would be plums, apples, and hops to pick. They lived by casual labor, and on their travels they bought, and sometimes stole, scrap metal, collected rags, and sold clothes-pegs and artificial flowers. This wasteland had been from time immemorial one of their "atchin tans," or stopping places. Being isolated and lonely, it posed little danger to them from police or angry landowners.

Now the silence of the wasteland was shattered as the travelers clambered out of their vehicles, and with practiced ease set about preparing for their stay. The children were dispatched to collect firewood. The women began to prepare the evening meal, and the men unhitched the caravans and checked that they stood level. In a very short space of time a big black cooking pot hung over a crackling fire, the goat was tethered and grazing contentedly, and the hens were pecking busily around and under the caravans. The family gathered around the fire, the men swarthy and dark-skinned, with gaudy neckerchiefs knotted about their throats. The women were burned brown by the sun, their auburn hair coiled in plaited ropes around their heads, and the flames from the fire glinted hungrily on the gold that hung from their ears, necks, and wrists. The children were ragged and dirty, but happy and well fed. They joked and gossiped among themselves for a while, and then one of the sons remembered the dogs, still cooped up in the back of the van.

He strolled over and opened the door, and they poured out in a joyous yelping stream. There were five of them, an ill-assorted crew, but each chosen and kept for his particular qualities. There was a great gray brute, the result of a mating between a collie and a greyhound, who could run down a hare in fifty yards. There was an Alsatian crossed with a retriever, who could bring back a partridge chick to the hand alive, so soft was his mouth, but who, when left on guard, was better than any lock. There were two whippets, who, working together, kept the family supplied with as many rabbits as they could eat and sell, and a tiny rough brown terrier who had earned his owner many a pound by killing rats. Free at last from the stuffy confines of the van, they raced around for a while, chasing each other's tails and engaging in mock combat, until at last, as their first euphoria waned, they settled down to explore their surroundings.

All this time Borun had lain in the thorn thicket, wide awake and anxious, listening to the tumult of sound that echoed over the wasteland. Although tempted to flee, he nevertheless remained where he was, waiting for darkness, for he was in strange country, and he had no idea which direction to take in search of safety. The likelihood of his being discovered seemed at first remote, for the undergrowth in the thorn thicket was prickly and dense, and there was little chance of a human forcing a way in. Then he heard the clamor of the dogs, the sound he hated most in all the world, and his heart sank.

The terrier found him first, and the hysterical yapping of the little dog brought the others to the scene. Borun set his back to the base of the ash tree and waited, his white teeth bared in a snarl of rage and defiance, confident that he could deal with both the terrier and the whippets, should they attempt to close with him. When the bigger dogs arrived, however, he knew that he was outnumbered, and taking a desperate chance, he screamed with anger and charged at the terrier.

The little dog yelped in fear and leapt aside, leaving Borun free to bolt. As the larger dogs floundered around, hampered by the clinging undergrowth, Borun burst through the thicket and shot out into the clearing like a hairy gray cannonball, only to stop short at the sight of the Romany family, sitting in a half-circle around the fire, and staring in amazement at the sudden appearance of the badger.

Borun hesitated only briefly. Then, as one of the men leapt to his feet and snatched up a heavy log, the badger swerved and ran for the woods. Yet even before he had covered a few yards he knew that he would never reach his goal, for the gray dog had broken free of the thicket and raced around to cut off Borun's escape. There was only one way for him to go. In a last desperate attempt to find sanctuary, he jumped through the open door of one of the caravans, while the dog, knowing full well the terrible penalty that awaited him from his master if he attempted to follow, stood and howled outside.

The man with the log moved forward, confident now that Borun was at his mercy. He was halfway through the door of the caravan when the older man cried out, "Wait!"

The son turned, scowling, but obedient to the command. "What now, father? What's there to wait for, when there's a badger pelt worth a five-pound note there for the taking, and badger hams to smoke over our fire?"

The father made a gesture of impatience. "You'd make a poor bargain if you did not wait. Could you trade your badger pelt for, say, six bottles of good whiskey?" He moved closer, laying his hand on his son's shoulder and continuing in a low, confidential voice. "I know a man, not far from here, who would give not one, but four five-pound notes for this badger, but it must be delivered alive, and in good condition."

The son thought about this for a few moments, then, throwing down his log, he carefully closed the caravan door, and sitting down on the step, squinted up at his father. "All right then. Who's this fool of a man who would part with so much money for an old badger, and why? Besides, how do you propose to take the brute alive? It'll tear you to pieces if you go near."

"Patience, patience," said the old man. "The man lives not far from here. He runs a kind of zoo, a wildlife park he calls it, and he charges tourists who come to see the animals. I sold him a litter of fox cubs in the spring, when we passed through, and he told me then that if ever I found a live badger, he would buy it. This one is no cub, but it is only a youngster, and if he doesn't want it, well, then will be the time to knock it on the head. As to taking it live, watch, and you will learn."

He moved over to the truck, and from out of the pile of scrap metal he pulled a length of iron piping, about five feet long and half an inch in diameter. Then from under the seat in the driver's cab he took a length of strong, thin cord. One end of the cord he knotted tightly to an end of the piping, and then threaded the cord down the tube, so forming a noose, which he drew tight several times to ensure that it ran freely.

Next he went to the wood and cut a long hazel wand, and came back trimming the twigs and leaves from it with his pocketknife. "Get me that strong wooden crate off the back of the wagon," he commanded his sons, "and bring me a hammer and some nails to fasten down the lid."

When all was ready he took the hazel wand in his left hand, and the pipe in his right, the noose hanging in a wide loop. Then, after instructing his sons to open the caravan door, and to place the crate in front of it after he had entered, he stepped inside the caravan.

Borun, crouched in a tiny space between the caravan's stove and a bunk bed, heard the sound of the door opening, and turned to face fresh danger. The old Romany advanced toward him, very slowly, taking step after careful step, the hazel wand pointing toward Borun, the loop of cord hung over the wand.

Borun watched the wand, for this seemed to him to offer the greater threat. He did not notice the noose, or paid no heed to it if he did. When the wand was within six inches of his snout he snapped, seizing the hazel between his jaws and sinking his teeth into the wood. Being green and pliant, it did not sheer off, but merely splintered between his jaws, and Borun hung on grimly as the old man pulled firmly but smoothly on the wand. While Borun's neck was thus stretched, and his teeth fully occupied, the noose slid down the wand and settled softly over his head. Next moment the man had pulled it tight.

Borun's scream died in his throat as he felt himself swung into the air. Choking, clawing at his neck, twisting, squirming, he was carried along and swung out of the caravan door.

The box was open, and he was lowered into it. As his feet touched the wooden floor the lid was clapped on, and darkness descended, but mercifully the cord around his neck suddenly slackened, and once more he was able to breathe. For a few seconds he was deafened by the banging of the hammer as the lid was nailed down, and then he was left in peace.

With the badger successfully captured, the Romanies settled down to their evening meal, and when it was over they loaded the crate into the back of the van and set off back down the road they had traveled earlier in the afternoon. The journey was short, but to Borun it was a nightmare of noise, and the stuffy confines of the crate were made worse by the combined smells of petrol, exhaust fumes, and the hateful smell of dog. At first he tried to claw and bite his way out of the crate, but it was new and strongly made, and he could make no impression on the unyielding wood. At last, exhausted and half suffocated, he lay down, his claws torn and bleeding, but he was too terrified to sleep.

At last the van stopped, and the engine was cut. Alert again, Borun waited and listened, but all he could hear were voices, which were meaningless to him. They went on for what seemed an interminable while, now raised, now low and pleading. Then the van door was opened, the crate was lifted out and carried away, Borun inside standing straddle-legged in order to keep his balance. The box was set down, the nails in the lid were drawn, and Borun fell in a heap as the box was turned suddenly on its side. Then the lid was pulled to one side, and light flooded in, light and sweet fresh air.

14. The Prisoners

Borun was in no hurry to leave the box, however unpleasant it was, for outside, he knew, the men were waiting. He could smell them, and hear their heavy breathing, and so he crouched motionless in a corner of the crate, preferring to endure any discomfort rather than face the unknown dangers that lay outside.

He was not left in peace for long. A stiff-bristled broom was pushed into the crate, and Borun was prodded with it. Borun snapped and tore at the bristles, but they pricked his lips and gums, and no matter how many he cut through with his sharp teeth, there were still more to torment him. The broom was like a live thing that would not bleed or suffer, and could not be vanquished. At last, Borun bolted from the crate.

Dazed and bewildered, Borun could see only that he was in a small enclosure, with smooth white walls and a concrete floor. He caught a brief glimpse of a pair of stoutly gaitered legs, guarded by the threatening broom, and then he spotted a pile of straw in a corner. He dived into it, burrowing down until he was lost to view, and the owner of the wildlife park, satisfied that he had a live badger in good condition, paid over the twenty pounds he had promised the Romanies. So the two men departed, well content with their evening's work.

The wildlife park, as it was called, had developed gradually over the years. At the end of the second world war a young army officer had bought a dilapidated mansion in the grounds of a small estate, with the intention of restoring the old house to its former grandeur. Purely as a temporary measure, he had moved into what had once been the head gardener's cottage, which stood in a walled garden, adjacent to the mansion. Now the old house was crumbling into ruin, and the officer, well past middle age, was still in the cottage.

At the end of the war building materials had been impossible to obtain, so to while away the time the young man had turned his attention to a small stream that flowed through the grounds, widening it and building several weirs. Then he fenced the water meadows into paddocks, and began to stock the stream with fish and wildfowl, ducks, geese, and swans. Gradually over the years he became more and more absorbed with his hobby, and as his interest grew, so his expenses became heavier, until one day, more to defray some of his costs than with any idea of making a profit, he opened his grounds to the public, advertising a riverside walk, and charging a modest entry fee.

The response took him totally by surprise, as thousands of visitors poured in on fine summer weekends. It was an age of affluence, and more and more people were acquiring cars, and the leisure to go touring. Bored and restless, they were eager for any diversion that came their way. So the riverside walk became a wildlife park. The rich brown loam of the kitchen gardens disappeared beneath lawns and gravel walks. The shrubberies were enclosed by aviaries, and the greenhouse became an aquarium and reptile house. The coach yard and stables became a children's corner, with Shetland ponies, goats, lambs and chickens, rabbits, cavies and doves all enjoying an indolent and more or less amicable existence. A restaurant was built, for the tourists arrived hungry and thirsty.

Gradually more exotic species made their appearance, and the green hills of England echoed to strange cries. A small herd of sea lions, never again to taste the salt spray of the Pacific Ocean, wallowed and splashed in the stream. An elderly lynx basked in the sun, and breathed air redolent of french fries and hamburgers instead of pine forests and muskeg swamps. A fish eagle from Africa brooded on the topmost branch of a dead pine stump, and ignored the blowflies that buzzed around the dried remains of a dead whiting lying on the floor of the cage. The animals were all well fed, and the cages clean and tidy, imaginatively designed to give the inmates the maximum of freedom and privacy, yet it seemed that an ineffable air of sadness hung over the grounds. Close by, the old mansion was settling slowly back into the earth. Plaster crumbled from the walls. Bats lived in the roof. A family of jackdaws nested in one of the chimneys, and a barn owl roosted in the tower.

Of late, the owner had conceived the idea of a section of the park devoted to mammals of the British Isles. To this end he had bought the fox cubs earlier in the spring, and he now had a badger. The arrival of Borun, however, had taken him by surprise, and since for the moment there was no suitable accommodation ready, Borun was temporarily housed in one of a new range of pigsties, from which there seemed no possibility of escape. Here the owner left Borun to recover from his ordeal, with a bowl of fresh water, and a dish of raw meat, together with two thick slices of bread plastered with honey.

Darkness fell, but Borun remained hidden in the straw pile. For a long time he stayed awake, trembling with fear and shock, but slowly his heart stopped hammering and his limbs ceased their twitching, and he slept. He woke a little before dawn and ventured out, feeling stiff and sore, but the water revived him, and he licked the honey from the bread before crawling back under the straw.

He slept but little during the following day, for the strange scents and the variety of noises that came to him continued to unnerve and bewilder him. Toward dusk he emerged again, and began to explore his surroundings.

The sty was divided into two parts, a sleeping compartment with a raised concrete platform, windowless and roofed over, and an outer yard, with walls four feet high, finished with a smooth rendering of plaster. The gate was solidly made of wood, clad with sheet steel and securely locked. There seemed to be no possible avenue of escape, but Borun persisted in his explorations, covering every inch of the enclosure, and from time to time standing on his hind legs and reaching high up the walls, in the hope of finding some foothold. There was none.

Yet unknown to the owner, the laborer who had built the pigsty had skimped the job. The specifications had called for two inches of sand and cement laid over two inches of hardcore, but in one corner of the sleeping compartment the covering was less than half an inch thick. The laborer had seen that he was about to run out of material. It was almost time for him to finish work, and he was too lazy to mix any more sand and cement, so he had filled the corner with loose earth and spread what mixture he had left thinly over it, confident that no one would notice.

In drying, the unequal thickness had caused the sand and cement to crack, but in the darkness no one had detected the flaw. Borun found it, and began to scratch.

Soon he discovered he could get his claws under the slab, and in response to his tugging it began to rock. Gradually he raised it until he was able to bite at the edge, and at last he could get his strong snout beneath it. Three quick jerks and the slab broke in two halves, which Borun dragged away, exposing the soft loose earth beneath. Now he began to dig in earnest, loosening the earth still further and dragging it back by the armful. Before long he was lost to sight, and the floor of the pigsty was covered with fresh soil.

He came to the foundations of the walls, and dug down until he had passed beneath them. Then he began to dig upward, making rapid progress, for the ground outside the wall had recently been excavated for the laying of the foundations, and shoveled back after the building had been completed. From time to time he rested, and once he took time off to return to the enclosure and drink the water provided, but he took no food. There was still an hour of darkness left before the dawn when he broke free of his prison, and emerged into the open.

The night was warm and windy, the stars hidden by a veil of cloud. Borun wandered around, seeking some way out of the walled garden, but each path he followed ended against a brick wall, a fence of chicken wire, or a cage whose startled occupant peered at him through the darkness. A porcupine rattled its quills. A great horned owl snapped its beak and crouched low on its perch. A roosting peacock awoke to screaming, flapping flight, and the old lynx ceased his endless prowling to growl a throaty warning. Borun's nerves were almost at breaking point when at last, quite by chance, he found the main entrance, and walked out under the turnstile.

A long winding drive stretched away across parkland studded with ancient elms and oaks. Borun hurried across the short tussocky grass, anxious to get as far away as possible from the wildlife park before dawn, and also to find some cover in which to spend the hours of daylight. Yet he knew that he could not travel far. A great weariness was on him, and a ravenous hunger, which was hardly surprising, for he had eaten little or nothing for three nights and days.

The parkland ended abruptly beside a main road, and here Borun was in luck, for the corpse of a rabbit lay still warm in the verge, where it had crawled after being struck by a passing car. Borun picked up the rabbit and hurried across the road with it dangling from his jaws, settling down to a late supper as soon as he was safely hidden in the bushes.

It was breaking light by the time he had finished eating, and the clouds of night were dispersing before a chill breeze that heralded the rising of the sun. Below him the hillside fell away in rolling heathland, a thick carpet of dark heather, interspersed by clumps of gorse, spindly birch trees, and here and there a stand of pine. Beyond the heathland lay a river, and beyond that a ridge of hills ending in a steep limestone escarpment. Something about the hills and the escarpment struck a chord in Borun's memory, but he paid no heed. He set off across the heathland. He had not gone far before he came upon a twisting narrow track that wound between the white stems of the heather. He stopped, and sniffed the ground carefully.

There was no doubt about it. Another of his kind had passed this way, and only a short while ago. For some reason he could not understand, the knowledge filled Borun with a strange excitement. He moved off down the trail, quickening his pace as the scent grew stronger, until he came to a hollow in the side of the hill, where the ground was bare of vegetation and sharp flints shone among the pale ocher of the gravel. At the foot of a twisted old gorse bush a hole had been dug, and the sweet musky aroma that had so excited and disturbed Borun hung all around it. He moved closer and called, and the constriction he felt at his throat half strangled what he had meant to be a whickering greeting, so that it emerged as a soft purr.

He waited, but no response came, so he called again, louder, and this time he heard a muffled padding deep in the earth. Respectfully, he drew back a little, continuing to call, but standing very still as cautiously, inch by inch, the other badger emerged. She was smaller than he, very trim and slender, and she stood blinking in the strong morning sunlight, one paw raised and her nose questing the air. Borun moved slightly, and for a moment she made as if to dive back into the hole, but then she came forward, until the two animals touched noses, and then sniffed each other over face, ears, and neck. Both badgers were trembling, he with eagerness and anticipation, she with slight fear and nervousness.

Then she turned, and made her way slowly back into the set. Borun stood outside, irresolute, anxious, wanting to follow but unsure of his welcome. He turned away, half determined to depart, to find some other shelter for the day, but then he heard her call, and saw that she was back at the mouth of the set, watching him and waiting for him to make the next move. He walked toward her, and she backed slowly away from him, leading him down out of sight, into the cool darkness of the set.

There was only one tunnel, quite short, but it led under a great slab of sandstone, and then widened out into a sleeping chamber lined with a deep litter of fern. Borun was vaguely conscious of her snuffling near him, and rustling the fern, and then a great wave of exhaustion swept over him, and he fell into a deep sleep.

15. Handa

The female's name was Handa. She had been born in the same year as Borun. She and her brother had left their parents' set the previous autumn, and for a while they had shared a home on this heathland. Then one night a month ago her brother had wandered away alone and failed to return. Since then she had led a solitary and none too happy existence. Several times she had been on the point of abandoning the set, to seek the company of other badgers. Now Borun had come into her life. The knowledge of his presence, as he slept beside her in the darkness, filled her with contentment, and she drowsed happily through the day.

It was late in the evening when Borun woke, to find himself alone in the sleeping chamber. Handa was waiting for him outside the set, and she trotted over to greet him as he emerged. The sun was setting, illuminating the sky in the northwest, and shedding a soft rosy luster over the shaggy cloak of the hillside. Together the two badgers lay on the bare baked earth, still warm from the sun's rays, listening and waiting as the first pale stars appeared and dusk stole out of the valley below, welling like a dark tide up the slopes of the hill. A few rooks flew lazily overhead, winging their way back to roost after a long day's toil in the fields, and an owl wafted low over the heather, dropping out of sight and then rising with a small burden clutched in one of its talons.

As if by tacit assent the pair rose and moved off downhill, Handa leading the way. Gradually the heather gave way to rough grassland, sour and ill drained, invaded by bracken and coarse rushes. Glow worms shone like fallen stars amid the grass stems, and white moths fluttered over the fern, to fade and vanish among the dark alders that lined the riverbank. Slugs and snails were feeding on the damp vegetation. The two badgers sought them out, selecting the fattest slugs and rolling them carefully to and fro on the grass until they had removed all the slime. It was a slow and painstaking business, but the badgers were in no hurry, and an hour passed as they worked their leisurely way across the marshy pasture.

They came at last to the river, where they paused to drink. There they disturbed a moorhen roosting in the reeds with her half-grown chick, sole survivor of a brood of seven. The mother flew out of the water, calling to her youngster to follow, but the witless bird panicked and ran away from the river. Handa gave chase, and Borun followed, driving it further into the field. Yet try as they might, they could not catch the moorhen chick, for no matter how foolish and hysterical it might be, it could easily outrun both of them. The chase became fast and furious, and more of a sport than a serious hunt for the badgers, so when at last the wretched bird dodged past Borun and plunged into the river, the pair watched it go without any great show of regret. They trotted along the riverbank together, side by side, jostling and pushing each other and pulling each other's ears. Gradually their play grew more boisterous and frenzied. Then, quite suddenly, they paused, and in that moment Borun made Handa his mate.

Their honeymoon lasted until late August, when all the wheat and barley had been harvested, and the fields lay tawny and sere under the maturing sun. They began to grow fat, gleaning the grain that had fallen on the stubble, and feasting on the blackberries that shone in juicy clusters of ripe black fruit in the hedgerows and thickets. They found mushrooms and other fungi, and from time to time a wasps' nest. All around them the earth burgeoned with wealth, as the full-blown beauty of the summer mellowed into misty autumn.

Then came the acorn crop. The hard fruit spattered down like hail from the high branches of the oaks, while from the chestnut trees fell spiky green purses, from which burst succulent, shiny brown nuts. This year too, the beechmast ripened, an uncommon event, and the squirrels that peopled the woodlands went quite silly burying far more of the seed than they could ever eat during the winter, even if they were able to find their stores again.

With the first frosts the bracken fern yellowed and died. When it was sufficiently withered and dry Handa raked out all the bedding from the set and replaced it with new, collecting great armfuls and dragging it down, until the bed chamber was packed to the ceiling with springy fresh material. She dragged the old bedding away from the vicinity of the set and scattered it among the heather, where it would decay and replenish the earth.

Although she was putting on weight, and three months had passed since she and Borun had consummated their union, there was as yet no sign that she was about to bear young.

Yet the alchemy of love that had brought them together was still at work within her, and all was well. The union of two animals is more, far more, than a mere physical mating. It is a moment when the forces of the universe, the slow traverse of the seasons, the long journey of the earth through space around the sun, the pull of the moon and the tides, all conspire to fuse in a flashpoint of desire; and this moment is but one in a carefully programmed cycle of events.

Neither Borun nor Handa had known another mate. Nor were they ever likely to, for badgers bond for life. Their coming together stimulated appetites which until then had remained dormant. There is little doubt that it was excitement and pleasure at Borun's company that caused Handa to ovulate.

Now three fertilized ova lay at rest in Handa's womb. They would remain dormant until the winter solstice, the longest night of the year, when her body would then accept and nourish them. Why all this should be so is a question to which there is as yet no answer. It is a mystery perhaps understood by the silent oaks beneath whose roots the badgers have so long survived, but it may forever elude the inquiry of man.

The purple plaid of the heather darkened to deepest brown, and the western gorse, which had worn a coronet of gold flowers, resumed its garb of somber green. Gales came, stripping the birch of its brassy leaves, and rain lashed the earth, turning the waters of the river to muddy beige, in which dark drowned alder leaves danced a slow and stately dance. Then the sun shone again, on a changed world, in which the nuances of color were soft and indistinct, a muted landscape of faded browns and greens, yet against which the wine purple of the bare birch twigs glowed, with a rare beauty that would pass unnoticed in a harsher light. At night a hunter's moon hung in a sky curtained with stars, and in the mornings frost rime silvered the skeletons of the flowers of summer.

Men armed with mattocks and spades came late one afternoon on a gray autumn day when mist hung over the river and moisture clung to every twig and dried fern and grass blade. They filled a plastic bag which had once held fertilizer with gravel and stuffed it down the mouth of the set. Then they shoveled more earth over the entrance, and stamped it down flat before they left.

A fox hunt was due to be held the next day, and the master was anxious that it should be a success. Previously there had been complaints from the farmers that foxes were getting too numerous, and hunt followers grumbled that too many escaped the hunt by going to ground. So the hunt committee had agreed to pay two laborers for the task of stopping as many holes as they could find, and although strictly speaking the holes should have been stopped up on the morning of the hunt, there were too many to be dealt with in the time available. So the two men privately agreed to find as many as they could on the previous day, and so avoid too early a start in the morning.

Borun and Handa heard the muffled thumping and banging as the earth stoppers did their work, but the sounds soon ceased, and as silence returned to the set the two badgers curled up in sleep once more. The atmosphere in the set grew hot and stuffy, but it was not for another two hours that the occupants were to discover that they were entombed.

It did not take Borun long to dig free. The plastic bag tore readily in his sharp claws, and the loose gravel spilled out. It took longer, once Borun had broken through, to clear the earth and gravel from the tunnel entrance, but long before the moon had risen above the crest of the hill the pair were off foraging. Yet Handa was nervous and uneasy, and twice during the night she returned to the set to check that all was well. Just before dawn they both retired to pass the day, but Handa remained restless and wakeful, listening at the entrance of the bedchamber.

So she was the first to hear the clamor of the hunt, and the deep belling voices of the hounds as they surged across the heath, close on the heels of a young dog fox that had led them down the valley and across the river. The fox was wet and bedraggled, his head and brush hung low, and his weary limbs faltered as he toiled across the coarse heather. Twice he had run to earth, only to find his escape route blocked by sticks and stones, and now he was making a last bid to find cover.

Handa heard the harsh rasp of his breathing as he slid into the tunnel, and her warning snarl brought him up short a yard from the sandstone slab beneath which the badgers lay. He moved forward cautiously, but then he heard Borun's voice in addition to Handa's, and knew he dare venture no nearer. To squeeze through the crevice, with two badgers on guard on the other side, would be to court certain death.

Now all three animals lay silent and still as they heard the frantic clamor of the hounds at the entrance to the set. They heard the thunder of hooves, shouting, and curses, and then silence, followed by a soft, low snuffling.

After roundly cursing all laborers who were not worthy of their hire, the master of foxhounds had ordered a terrier to be sent down the hole. The little dog went in eagerly enough, and after a moment the assembled hunt heard its excited yapping as it came face to face with the fox. An old huntsman dismounted, and put his ear to the ground. Rising, he shook his head, and moved a yard or so further on, to kneel and listen again. Then he nodded, and tapped the ground beneath his heel, as an indication as to where to dig.

For the second time in twenty-four hours, Borun and Handa heard the thump and clink of spades, and soon after, the rattle of loose earth into the tunnel. They did not see the fox hauled out and thrown to the waiting hounds, and his death scream was drowned beneath the triumphant yelping of his tormentors. Loose earth blocked the entrance to the bedchamber, and no one paid the slightest heed to the little terrier still scratching in the tunnel.

The day was rapidly drawing to a close. Everyone was bone tired, cold, and hungry, and for many there was a long hack home, horses to be fed and watered and bedded down for the night, hounds to be tended to, and harness cleaned and dried before there was any chance of a bath and a meal. Most of the hunt followers agreed that after such a fine run, the digging out of the quarry was somehow a distasteful anticlimax, a necessary job to be done, but one which somewhat soured the day. One by one they left the field. The hounds were whipped in, and the terrier, which was still scratching in the tunnel, was hauled out by the scruff of his neck and thrown across a saddle.

As the last light faded from the land, the hill lay deserted, dark, and unchanged save for the ruins of the badger set, which yawned like an open grave. Close by, on the heather, there was a patch which from a distance resembled a scattered tribute of dark red roses, rapidly turning black in the fast gathering dusk.

16. The Long Journey

Borun and Handa waited for a long time after the hunt had left before they dared try to venture out of the blocked bedchamber, and it was only then that they discovered that freedom was not to be gained merely by scraping away a few armfuls of loose gravel. A large block of sandstone, which had once formed part of the roof of the tunnel, had fallen across the entrance, and was held in place by loose earth which the terrier had been unable to scratch away.

The block was too big to drag through the crevice, and too firmly embedded in the earth to be pushed aside. It took many hours of patient scraping and burrowing, dragging soil and small stones, a pawful at a time, into the sleeping chamber, before Handa was at last able to squeeze through, and past the rock. Then she was able to dig from outside, and it was not long before Borun could push aside the rock and crawl free.

Outside, in the fresh damp air, the badgers shook themselves vigorously, to free themselves of the loose particles of soil that covered their coats. Then, although they were weary, hungry, and thirsty, they began a slow and meticulous inspection of their home. The set was ruined beyond repair. The tunnel had caved in, and the sleeping chamber was drafty and exposed. Everywhere the ground was redolent of the smell of fox, hounds, horses, and humans, defiled and polluted to a degree that repelled both animals. When Handa found the remains of the fox on the heather, it was the last straw. With a gruff bark of anger and dismay she bolted away downhill, and Borun followed at a gallop, anxious not to lose track of her.

Once clear of the vicinity of the set, Handa quieted somewhat, and Borun began to forage for food. Soon Handa joined him. When Borun unearthed a cache of acorns, buried by a squirrel in the leafmold under the parent oak, she ate heartily of the fruit and began to forget the tragedy that had passed. Neither animal had any intention of returning to the ruined set, but they were not unduly concerned about the problem of finding shelter. Each knew every detail of the countryside around the set, and could call to mind half a dozen suitable refuges: holes dug by foxes and referred to as "earths" by the country folks, abandoned badger sets, and passages under the sandstone rocks that littered the hills. Even some of the older rabbit warrens had tunnels wide enough and spacious enough to accommodate them. So it was not until an hour before the dawn that Handa led the way up the side of the hill, to where, she knew, a fault in the eroded rock face allowed access to a dry and roomy cavern.

It was no good. The entrance had been blocked with a massive slab of stone, which had required the combined efforts of the two earth stoppers to lever into place. Handa scratched and pushed at the stone for a few minutes, then turned away, heading downhill to the site of an old quarry, in the corner of which a vixen had dug an earth and raised her young. The earth had long since been abandoned, and no taint of fox remained, but here again Handa was disappointed, for once more the earth stoppers had done their work well. A tree stump had been thrust into the mouth of the hole, and loose earth and stones heaped over it. Given time, the badgers might well have cleared the blockage, but daylight was fast approaching, and both animals were bone weary.

Now Borun led the way, to an earth mound that lay in the middle of a small beech wood. The mound was an ancient grave, the tomb of a Bronze Age chieftain who had been laid to rest there, with his weapons and his jewelry, with clay pots filled with food, and rich garments of wool and fur to keep him warm on his journey to the other land. There was a way into the tomb, Borun knew, at the base of the oldest beech tree, and when last he had visited it, there had been a spider's web spun across the entrance, a sure sign that it was deserted.

The hole was still there, and it had been overlooked by the earth stoppers, but there was no spider, and no web. Instead there was an old and irascible badger, driven half mad with toothache and pains in his joints, who was in no mood to welcome others of his kind, however great their need of shelter. He stood just inside the entrance to the tomb, growling and snarling, and Borun, who was quite big enough and powerful enough to master the old warrior, hovered timidly outside, wheedling and cajoling, in the hope of being allowed in. It was all to no avail, and Borun and Handa turned away. They could not ignore those instincts that taught them to respect the territorial rights of others. They left the tomb, and its testy old custodian backed off, muttering, into the dark recesses. Soon, his bones would join those of the other old warrior, and their spirits would become as one.

It was full daylight when the pair finally found refuge, in a small cave at the foot of a low sandstone cliff. A dense mat of ivy hung down the rock face, screening the entrance to the cave, and so the earth stoppers had missed it, too. Yet it was a poor sort of refuge, drafty and damp and cold, and the badgers lay huddled together on a bed of loose stones, in the driest corner they could find. For a while they forgot their discomfort in sleep, but nightfall found Borun wakeful and restless, padding to and fro at the entrance to the cave and looking out, beyond the ivy curtain, across the valley to where the limestone escarpment was stark against the winter sky.

Something about the shape of the hill pulled at his mind, evoking half-forgotten memories of a valley and a wood, a wood where it seemed it was always summer, and the voles were fat and sweet and plentiful, where rabbits ran among the fern and no man came near. As soon as darkness fell he left the cave and set off toward the river, moving purposefully down the wooded hillside without pausing to search for food. Handa followed, not knowing where she was going or why, but content merely to go with her mate.

Borun himself had no clear intention, no positive plan. He knew only that as long as he traveled toward the hills, he felt satisfied and content. The moment he stopped, or turned aside, his restlessness returned. So he journeyed on, until at last he was brought up short by the broad expanse of the river, now brown and turbulent with the winter rains.

Here he checked. Then, on impulse, he turned right and followed the river upstream. With every step he felt he was going more and more astray, and after a hundred yards or so he turned, retracing his steps, still following the river but heading downstream, and immediately he felt better. Handa plodded behind, as patient and trusting as ever.

Without map or compass to guide him, Borun's instinct led him true. After his capture by the Romanies, he had without knowing it been carried across the river in the van. Now it lay before him, sprawled like a great snake across the valley floor, swinging in wide curves as it meandered down to the sea. But it lay aslant his path rather than across it, and by heading downstream Borun was in fact drawing nearer to his goal, even though he was traveling at a slight tangent to it. How he was going to cross the river was a problem which had not even occurred to him.

The going was easy, along a wide track worn bare by the booted feet of countless fishermen, and the pair made good progress until Handa rebelled. A tree trunk lay beside the path, its bark crumbling and rotten. Rich yellow clusters of fungi clung to the decaying wood, and moss hung in trailing green tendrils, on which beads of moisture glistened in the starlight. The thought of all the food hidden under the bark was too much for Handa, and she called a halt in order to feed.

Borun, once his interest was aroused, was happy to join her, for his earlier restlessness had now much abated. Together they ripped the log apart, licking up the gray wood-lice that scattered in all directions, and crunching the colonies of snails that were hibernating there. Beneath the bark, in the spongy timber, lay the fat white grubs of boring beetles, and best of all, in the soft ground under the log, they found a congregation of frogs, deep in their winter sleep.

His hunger appeased, Borun was once more ready to move, but Handa felt certain that yet a further treat lay in store beneath the log. She lingered for some minutes, searching in vain, while Borun bickered and chivied her, anxious to be off. She gave in after a while, and followed Borun along the path, grumbling to herself a little, but obedient to his will.

Ahead of them now the river was spanned by a bridge, but to gain access to the bridge they had to climb a high earthen rampart, that lay at right angles to their path. Together the pair clambered up the bank, some twenty feet or more in height, and found themselves on a wide level track. Two parallel steel rails ran along the length of the track, shining dully in the starlight, and Borun approached them nervously, with Handa close behind. He was halfway across the first rail when he realized that it was singing, and the song, a high-pitched whine, grew steadily louder, accompanied all the while by a rhythmic clicking sound.

Borun started back, almost bowling Handa over in his fright, and the pair of them retreated crouching in the thick dry grass as the whine grew to a hurricane of sound, a deafening roar and a whistle, together with a mighty pounding that made the earth shake. As they watched, too terrified to move, the train thundered past, the lights from the carriage windows flicking over their faces as they crouched low to the ground. Then it was gone. The noise faded into the distance, and then died.

It was more than half an hour before Borun and Handa dared venture once more onto the railway track, and this time they approached the rails with even more caution than before. The rails were silent, however, and Borun led the way across the bridge and over the river. Fortune was with them, for if Handa had not lingered that extra while at the tree stump, the train would have caught them halfway across the bridge, and probably killed them both.

The two badgers followed the railway for about half a mile, until it joined another track running roughly east to west. Borun hesitated only briefly before crossing the track, sliding over the smooth shining rails that lay in orderly rows before him. Once again, fortune favored him, for had the line been electrified, he would have died immediately. They slid down the embankment, crossed a small field, and pushed through the hedge, only to be caught up short by another obstacle, a broad stretch of water extending interminably in either direction.

Years ago, men had cut the canal across the country, to link two ports, and for a time it carried a heavy volume of traffic. Barges towed by horses ferried coal and timber, iron ore and hides, all manner of imperishable goods, especially fragile articles, such as pottery, which would not stand a jolting journey over the rough roads of that time. Then came the railway, swifter by far, and slowly, the canal fell into disuse. The locks crumbled and decayed, and nature came to reclaim her own. In summer water lilies carpeted the surface of the water, and flag irises bloomed along the banks. Birds nested amid the rushes, and fat tench lay basking in the sunlit shallows. Each autumn the weeds died down, to decay into thick black mud. Slowly, very slowly, the canal was being filled up, and there would come a day when it would once more be dry land.

Both railway and canal had been cut as nearly as possible in a straight line along the valley through which the river wandered, crossing and recrossing the natural waterway, and forming a pattern which resembled a gigantic dollar sign. Yet in spite of all their care in planning, the engineers were bound from time to time to follow natural contour lines, to avoid the expense of cuttings and embankments. So Borun found himself on a stretch of canal running due east to west, and was at a loss to know whether he should go left or right.

In the end he turned east again, following the overgrown towpath that led along the side of the canal. Withered sedges rustled in the breeze, a moorhen called anxiously as they approached, and swam away from the shore. A sleeping swan awoke, and raised his long white neck to hiss at them as they passed, and a water vole dived into the water with a musical plop. Then Borun stopped, listening.

All this while his mind had been recording the noises of the night, decoding them and classifying them as harmless, but now he had picked up one which refused to be categorized. It came again, from the middle distance, and just around a bend, a splashing sound. He waited, but the long seconds ticked by, and there was no repetition of the noise, so he moved on. Then it came again, louder this time, and nearer, as though some vast bulk had reared out of the water and fallen back. Handa was visibly nervous, and ready to flee, but for the moment Borun stood his ground, waiting and listening, trying to determine what manner of beast it might be that lived in the canal.

He did not have to wait long. There was an upheaval in the shallow water near the bank. A great head appeared, with monstrous ears crowned by a wreath of rotting, mud-stained weed, and behind that the indeterminate bulk of some huge body. Handa fled, with Borun close behind, and the pig, which had escaped from his sty to enjoy the luxury of a midnight bath, gazed after their fleeting forms in mild surprise.

Again, it was in a way fortunate that the badgers had met the pig. Had they carried on the way they were going, they would have crossed an aqueduct, and in due course they would have found themselves back on the other side of the river. As it was, they came shortly to a narrow bridge, which led them across the canal, and into a small copse. Here they found a rich harvest of wild hyacinth bulbs, and they dug the crisp juicy roots from the soft mold, feeding until dawn whitened the sky, and forced them to seek refuge in a hollow log.

With the coming of the night Borun was again restless and anxious to be on the move, but Handa insisted on feeding first. For a while Borun joined her, but as soon as his appetite was appeased the urge to travel grew strong in him again, and he bullied and nagged at his mate until at last she followed him out of the wood.

The direction he had to take was now strong and clear in Borun's mind, but the way was not easy. After crossing several fields they came to a busy highway, and when they had successfully negotiated this hazard they found themselves in a narrow lane. High banks topped with sheep fencing kept them from gaining access to the fields on either side, and once a passing car braked and swerved to avoid them as they darted in panic across the road.

The lane led them to Summercombe village. The badgers wandered through a maze of gardens, past darkened cottages where dogs barked from behind closed doors, one so loudly and persistently that a light appeared at an upstairs window and a man's head appeared. Deep in the shrubbery by the garden wall Borun and Handa froze, not daring to move until the window banged shut and the light went out.

Once clear of the village, their troubles were over. Borun led the way uphill, through fields and hedgerows, until he came to a rough tangle of fern and stone. Here he stopped, to sniff the air appreciatively, before leading Handa around the edge of the hill fort, and into Summercombe wood.

A few minutes later they arrived at the set. All was well. One Eye had long since departed, and time, together with the industry of innumerable scavengers, had all but obliterated the traces of her brief tenancy. Although some of the smaller entrances had caved in, the tunnels were largely intact. After a thorough exploration, Handa set about clearing up the main sleeping chamber, raking the old debris and dragging it out of the set. Beneath the trees there was dried fern in plenty, and deep drifts of leaves, crisp, brown, and fragrant, which Handa dragged into the set until the sleeping chamber was full. Long before dawn the set was habitable again. The badgers had returned to Summercombe wood.

17. Parenthood

It was the time of the winter solstice. As the path of the planet earth drew ever nearer its sun the north pole leaned away, sheltering its icy wastes from heat and light under a veil of darkness. At the hour of the perihelion, when the north star blazed with white fire over a land chilled with frost, and the tall trees stood silent and still, Handa's body accepted the dormant eggs within her and began to nourish them with her blood.

She was not aware of any change within her, and the month of January passed, cold and bleak, with icy winds from the east holding the land in thrall. In February the wind blew from the west, turning the snow to a gray blanket of slush that vanished in a night, save for a few drifts that lay lost and forgotten in the sunless hollows of the hills. A thrush shouted from the topmost branch of an ash tree, and the plump catkins on the willow shone silver in the sun.

One evening, as the sun blazed blood red beneath massed banks of cloud, suffusing the white petals of the wood anemones with rosy pink, Handa emerged alone from the set and disappeared into the prickly thicket of holly that grew close by. A rabbit, long dead, had once dug a burrow under the roots of the parent holly tree, and Handa began to scratch and dig, enlarging the hole so that it was just big enough for her to squeeze into.

Digging was easy in the soft sand, and she was already well underground when Borun sleepily emerged, to sit scratching himself at the mouth of the set. He could hear Handa at work in the holly thicket, but he paid little heed. Digging was second nature to the badgers, and they were both frequently at work, clearing debris out of a tunnel where the roof had partially caved in, or enlarging a sleeping chamber because it was too cramped. For the moment Borun was content to lie at the mouth of the set, waiting for Handa to join him on the night's forage.

After two hours had passed, however, he began to grow impatient, and padded over to the holly thicket. Deep underground he could hear a muffled thumping and a rattling of loose stones, but when he tried to enter the tunnel he found it was too narrow for his bulk. He withdrew his head, and the next moment he was pushed aside by Handa as she emerged backward, dragging a large stone in her arms.

He called to her, but she ignored him, bustling away down the tunnel, to reappear almost at once with an armful of sand, most of which, when she scattered it, went over Borun. He withdrew out of range, and settled down to wait once more, but it was late in the night, and the moon was westering, before she condescended to join him in a search for food.

She was hard at work again the following night when

Borun woke, and this time he did not wait for her, but went off foraging alone, returning from time to time to call for her, until at last she was ready to join him. By midnight on the third night she had finished her task, and when Borun appeared, she was taking in bedding.

The nursery she had dug was a model of its kind. The entrance under the holly tree was small and discreet, the excavated soil scattered and lost under the dense canopy of dark evergreen leaves. Just inside, it took a right-angle turn, sloping slightly upward to pass between two rocks. Again it turned through ninety degrees, this time to the left, still sloping uphill but leading deep into the earth. A step up, over a slab of stone, and then down into a nursery chamber from which no cub could stray, and to which no harm could come, especially with Handa on guard. The slab of sandstone rock was a vantage point from which she could drop on any intruder.

Not until the nest chamber was lined to her satisfaction did Handa consent to join Borun in foraging, and even then she would not stray far. Long before dawn she led the way back to the set, but instead of following Borun into their sleeping chamber, she vanished quietly into the nursery. Borun waited a while, but she did not reappear, so he retired to sleep alone. The following evening he called to her at the mouth of the nursery set, but there was no response, so he padded off alone into the darkness beneath the trees. He was not to know it, but he was the father of three lusty cubs, two female and one male.

From the moment of their birth, the cubs flourished under Handa's tender care. She was able to feed them well, for she was young and healthy, and although January had been a lean month, for the rest of the year the land had been kind to her. On the first night she took no food, apart from the afterbirths she had devoured, but thirst troubled her, and a little before dawn she went to the spring to drink. On the second night she met Borun, and the pair exchanged a brief greeting before she returned to her young. On the third night she joined him for a short foray, and ever after that, on mild evenings, she would leave her cubs for a brief spell while she foraged with her mate through the woods.

By the middle of March she had decided that the nursery was no longer big enough to accommodate her brood, and she took over part of the main set, refurbishing an old abandoned sleeping chamber for the purpose. Some excavation was needed, and in digging, she turned out some old bones, yellow and crumbling with age. One was a skull, the teeth long fallen from the sockets, and Borun sniffed at it curiously as it lay on the sand outside the set. It was the skull of his great-grandfather, who had died in that very bedchamber, and who had been walled in by a sorrowing widow almost thirty years previously.

Once the new nursery had been furnished to her satisfaction, Handa brought her cubs across, one by one. So Borun met his family for the first time, and though at first Handa would not let him touch the cubs, and snarled a warning at him when he tried to enter the nursery, she gradually relaxed her rules. By now the cubs were snub-nosed miniatures of their parents, tottering about the nursery on rubbery little legs, and Borun was able to play nursemaid, allowing the youngsters to tug at his ears and hair, while Handa took a much-needed respite above ground.

There was no shortage of food. The rabbits and voles were breeding more than ever before, and although the spring was cold and dry there was a good yield of fresh green grass. During the drought of the previous summer every tree and shrub had thrust their roots deep into the earth, searching for water, and inadvertently tapping rich new sources of minerals in their quest. Now they were reaping the benefit of the hot, dry weather, and every tree, as it blossomed, showed promise of a heavy fruit crop to follow. The yellow catkins of the hazel were thicker and longer than ever before in the memory of man. The blackthorn bloom spread like snow over the land, and the flowers of the oaks, which normally passed unnoticed, flourished until the trees looked as if they had been sprayed with liquid gold.

For some time now Farmer Fletcher had been suffering more and more from a progressive disease of the hip joints, which made walking tedious and painful. His doctors had promised him that in time an operation could be performed, which would remove the pain, but meanwhile he would have to wait until the condition developed beyond a certain stage.

The daily routine grew increasingly arduous, and while he managed to cultivate the flat lands adjacent to the farm, Fletcher found the hilly fields too steep to climb. So, gradually, the green fields began to return to forest, the forest that had flourished for thousands of years before the coming of the first farmer, and which may one day flower over the bones of the last. Slowly the bracken fern invaded the pastures, and the bramble thickets spread outward, providing shelter for seedling thorn trees and wild briars, which in turn created food and shelter for small birds and beasts.

On a warm afternoon in late April, a boy toiled across the slope of the hill. He was tall for his age, and skinny, with bony elbows and knees and thin red wrists that stuck out from the sleeves of his sweater. A solitary child, his interest lay in birds and insects and flowers rather than conventional sports and pastimes, and so he shunned his schoolfellows, preferring to rake the mud at the bottom of a field pond in search of aquatic insects, or to comb the hedgerows for birds' nests. These habits, together with his appearance, made him an object of ridicule among his peers, and so he grew shyer and more alone than ever, preferring to follow the lanes and byways, and hiding or running away whenever he met one of his tormentors.

His proudest possession was a small museum and zoo,

which he kept in a shed at the bottom of his garden. Here he tended his specimens of pond life, contained in an array of glass jars. Here he also kept a live bank vole and a dormouse, and an owl with an injured wing. His great fear in life was that one day his father would carry out his threat to "pour all that rubbish down the drain." His mother was neutral. She avoided the garden shed and the unmentionable horrors that lay within.

He wore a small haversack, in which he carried what he called the tools of his trade: a magnifying glass and a notebook, a pair of tweezers and a trowel, an assortment of plastic bags and a knife, some pieces of string, and other odds and ends. There was also a fine-mesh net on a wire frame, which, if necessary, he could fit onto the long handle he carried in his right hand, and used as a walking stick. Fear of ridicule inhibited him from carrying the net ready assembled, even in so isolated a spot as this.

He had walked a long way, and he was hot and tired and thirsty, but there was no shade, and no fruit or berries to quench his thirst. Ahead lay the wood, and the dappled shade of the budding trees looked cool and inviting. Perhaps, too, there might be a stream or a spring from which he could drink. Questing along the hedge in search of entry he came upon the badger track, and it was easy for him, with his stature, to squeeze through the gap and follow the trail.

It led him to the spring, where he drank gratefully, before stripping off his boots and bathing his feet in the ice cold water. Resting thus, and reclining against the rock, he noticed the pad marks in the mud of the soft ground around the spring. He examined them carefully, unsure as to what species of mammal had made them. A solemn boy who was very serious about his hobbies, he took out his notebook and made a sketch, exactly lifesize. He also made a note to obtain some plaster of Paris, so that he could return and make plaster casts of the prints. Then he dried his feet on a handkerchief and put his boots back on, before following the trail further into the wood.

As soon as he saw the badger set he recognized it for what it was, and the origin of the prints became clear. Although he had never seen a badger, nor stumbled across a set before, he had read about them in the natural history books in his school library. Thrilled at his discovery, he poked about in the sand thrown up at the mouth of the main entrance, and soon found the skull of Borun's ancestor, which he stowed in his haversack. He found several black and white hairs too, shed from Borun's shaggy coat, and these he placed carefully between the leaves of his notebook. Finally he drew a sketch of the set, showing the entrances in relation to trees and rocks, and with an arrow indicating north. At last, regretfully, he moved on, knowing that the badgers would not emerge until dusk, and that to stay away from home for so long might cause his father to carry out his dread threat.

He came to a small clearing among the trees, a lush green glade of grass with a solitary ash sapling sprouting in the center. A movement on the edge of the clearing caught his eye and he froze, watching and waiting to see what manner of creature he had discovered. There was a rustling of dried leaves, and then a small gray form appeared, with a bright dark eye. At first the boy thought it was just a rabbit, but then he saw the bushy waving tail and realized that it was a gray squirrel. As he watched, it ran a few paces out into the clearing and then sat bolt upright, its tail curled like a question mark as it held some tidbit in its forepaws, and nibbled at it with its bright orange teeth.

The gray squirrel had been introduced into Britain from North America many years before the boy had been born. He had read how the gray squirrel had spread through the country, and knew that it caused some damage to forestry, but guessed, rightly, that many reports were exaggerated. He had read, too, that the gray squirrel had somehow driven out the native red variety, but more recently he had learned that the red squirrel had been growing rare before the advent of the gray, and that destruction of the old primitive forests was more likely to be the cause of its extinction.

All the same, he knew that the gray squirrel was not popular with owners of woodland, and simultaneously the thought came to him that it might be fun to keep the gray squirrel as a pet, and teach it to sit on his shoulder. The squirrel was now near the base of the ash sapling, busily foraging among the grass at its roots, and it occurred to the boy that if he were to startle the squirrel, it would instinctively climb the tree, and from there he could shake it down onto the grass, and then grab it. No sooner had the idea occurred to him than he put it into practice, letting out a wild yell and rushing into the clearing.

The squirrel did just as he expected, leaping up into the tree and climbing to the top, and next moment the boy was shaking the tree violently. For a few seconds the squirrel held on, and then, losing its grip, it fell, snatching frantically at branches on the way down, gaining momentary holds, but finally landing asprawl in the grass at the boy's feet. As it began to leap away the boy laid hold of it, one hand clutching it tightly around the neck, and the other gripping its haunches.

18. Thomas Slips Back

For a few moments the squirrel lay limp, temporarily paralyzed with shock and fear, and the boy had time to feel the soft, warm, rounded curves of the small body, and the silkiness of its fur. Unconsciously he relaxed his grip a little, and the squirrel, sensing this, twisted violently in his hand, and sank its chisel-like teeth deep into the fleshy ball of his thumb.

The boy screamed in pain, and tried to throw the squirrel to the ground, but the squirrel held on, its teeth locked together in the boy's flesh. In panic now, the boy tried to shake his attacker off, but the squirrel, twisting and writhing, refused to let go, until at last its teeth tore through the skin, leaving a raw and jagged hole from which blood poured in a steady stream.

Free at last, the squirrel began to leap away through the long grass, but the boy, half mad with pain and rage, pursued it, lashing out at it with his foot. His boot caught the squirrel behind the ear, so that it screamed and died, and at that moment the boy's rage left him. He fell on his knees beside the still palpitating corpse, and with his uninjured hand tried to massage life back into the small body, praying all the while that it was only stunned, but knowing that it was beyond saving.

Had anyone told him that morning that later in the day he would wantonly destroy an animal, his reaction would have been one of stunned disbelief. Even now, he could not understand what had happened. Grief, remorse, and pain from his injured hand all fused in an agony of despair that could find outlet only in an outburst of weeping, and thus Polly found him as she burst into the clearing.

The warm spring sunshine had lured her away from her garden to wander into the woods for an hour, and she had heard the boy scream as the squirrel bit him. Long experience with children had taught her to distinguish between the normal range of whoops and yells and a genuine cry of pain or terror. She knew that something was seriously wrong, and so she had at once hurried to the spot. She could not at first understand what had happened, but she could see that he was in no immediate danger, so she knelt down beside him and laid one arm over his shoulder. The boy ignored her, and continued to sob.

"Come on, young fellow," she said gently. "Dry your eyes and tell me your name. Have you got a handkerchief?"

Dumbly, the boy fumbled in his pocket and produced a very dirty rag. Polly smiled wryly, wondering how after all her years as a schoolteacher she could be so stupid as to ask a boy such a question. Then she saw the wound on his hand.

"Come on," she said, "this won't do at all. I'll take you to my home and fix that hand."

Without protest, the boy allowed her to raise him to his feet, and followed her obediently through the wood to the cottage. Polly took him into the kitchen and sat him down in a chair while she bustled about with a bowl of warm water and her first-aid kit, and ten minutes later his wound was dressed and swathed in a snow-white bandage. Then she bathed his tear-stained face with fresh cold water and poured him a glass of milk. "Now," she said brightly, "tell me your name."

The wave of emotion had passed, but the boy was still white and trembling with shock. "It's, it's Thomas, Miss. I, I didn't mean to do it."

"Do what?" queried Polly. "I'm still not sure what happened. Tell me about it."

Slowly, hesitantly, Thomas told her what had happened, the tears springing afresh to his eyes at the recollection, tears now of shame and guilt. Polly listened in silence until he had finished and sat staring at the kitchen floor.

"Tell me a bit more about yourself," Polly said. She wanted time to reflect. She recalled vividly, as if it were yesterday, the sudden attack by a young badger on a defenseless hedgehog, and it seemed to her that there was a parallel here somewhere. "Tell me about your school, and your hobbies. What were you doing in the wood today?"

Bit by bit Thomas began to tell her of his likes and dislikes, and soon he was describing his museum and zoo, and showing her his notebook. As he talked about his hobbies he grew more enthusiastic, and his face became flushed and animated. Polly was particularly interested in his account of the badger set. She had not herself ventured so far into the wood, so she had not discovered the set for herself. Now she found herself wondering whether this was the home of the young badger she had fed two autumns ago. She was on the point of telling Thomas about this when she suddenly realized that he had become crestfallen and silent again, and guessed he was thinking about the squirrel.

"I think you have reproached yourself enough about what happened this afternoon," she said kindly. "I think you just slipped back for a moment."

"Slipped back?" echoed Thomas. "How do you mean, Miss? Slipped back to where?"

"Back to the days of your ancestors," answered Polly. "Once, many thousands of years ago, our ancestors were hunters, roaming the hills and woods, just as you were this afternoon, only they were searching for food, and if they had found a squirrel, as you did, they would have reacted in exactly the same way. Only," she added, "they would have been more careful not to get bitten."

The boy shook his head. "But I don't like killing. I've never killed anything before, and I certainly won't ever again."

"No, I don't think you will," replied Polly slowly. "But don't you see, you are still a hunter, only now you hunt knowledge instead of food. You no longer have any need to kill, and the more you learn about the lives of other creatures, the less you want to kill them, but just for a moment, out there in the wood this afternoon, pain and shock made you lose control. You forgot who and what you were, and reverted back to your ancestry. Instinct told you what to do, and you did it without question, even though it was strictly against your principles. In future, now you know the enemy within you, you will have more control."

She paused for breath, and for a silent prayer that she was right. Still, deep down she felt confident that she had read young Thomas correctly. Whether he had understood half of what was said to him was another matter.

But Thomas was nodding his head solemnly. "I didn't want to kill the squirrel," he said. "But I wanted to own it, to keep it, and that's nearly as bad as taking its life. Taking its freedom, I mean. I have no right to do that. I was so stupid. Next time I feel like doing something like that I'll remember the squirrel, and stop and think.''

"Then perhaps the squirrel did not die in vain," said Polly. "Come on. I'll drive you home. Only I think, if anyone asks, we'll just say the squirrel fell out of a tree, and you got bitten when you went to pick it up. That's nearly the whole truth, and the rest will be our secret."

She drove Thomas down to the village, and gave a brief explanation of the afternoon's events to the boy's mother, a vague, harassed woman who seemed to stare vacantly into space all the time she was talking to her. After extracting a rather half-hearted promise from her that she would take Thomas to a doctor to have his hand dressed properly, Polly hurried away.

On the way back to the cottage she found her thoughts turning toward the badger set that Thomas had described to her. She now knew roughly where it was, and though it was too late in the day to go search for it, she resolved to go exploring first thing the next morning.

A bright day dawned, with a blustery wind from the northwest sending white clouds scudding across a sky as blue as a thrush's egg, and setting the leaves of the oak trees to dance and shimmer in the sunlight. Small brindle butterflies hovered and floated over the young nettle plants, and bees were busy among the white star flowers of the wild garlic. Polly found herself wondering if the resulting honey would be garlic flavored.

She walked on, through the sun-dappled shade of the woodland, breathing the heavy perfume of the wild hyacinths, the leaves of the previous autumn crisp and dry underfoot. She came to the badger track and followed it, as it twisted and wound under the trees. Once she had to crouch down to pass through a low tunnel of blackthorn, and once she had to scramble over a fallen tree. The badger track itself passed under the trunk, and Polly noticed how smooth and worn the bark was at that spot.

At length the track opened out into a wide arena beneath the trees, and Polly saw the yawning mouths of the entrances to the tunnels, black in the morning light. She did not go near them, but instead circled around until she was above them, seeking about her for a vantage point to which she could return that evening, when she hoped to see the badgers emerge into the open. She found it in an old ash stump, shaped for all the world like a large armchair, with back and arm rests, and even a footstool. All it needed to make it really comfortable was a cushion, and that was easily arranged.

She devoted the rest of the day to her garden, finishing off the last of the spring planting, hoeing between the tall green spires of the onions, and staking the peas newly emerging from the soil. Although slapdash and untidy in her housekeeping, she was almost fanatically orderly and neat in her vegetable plot. The beds were raked and rolled to billiard-table smoothness, the seeds set in exactly parallel rows, and the young plants spaced with mathematical precision. Not a weed was permitted to survive.

So the time passed, with one task suggesting and leading to another. The afternoon was well spent when the sudden appearance of Vandal, the white cat, reminded Polly that once again she had forgotten to collect the milk from the farm. For a moment she was tempted to go without it, but she knew that Vandal would expect his daily ration, and if he did not get it, he would spend the evening rubbing around the refrigerator and miaowing at the top of his voice. With a sigh, Polly put away her gardening tools and set off to the farm.

Mrs. Fletcher greeted her with that subdued air of triumph that befits the bearer of grave but important news. "Have you seen the papers, Miss Shaw?" she trumpeted, as Polly crossed the farmyard. She was confident that Polly had not. She took no papers whatsoever, as Mrs. Fletcher well knew. That was why she had waited impatiently all day for this moment.

Polly allowed herself to be led into the farm kitchen, where the front page of the *Advertiser* lay displayed for her to see. There was no doubt as to which news item had aroused Mrs. Fletcher. Glaring banner headlines leapt out of the page: NEW BY-PASS PROPOSED. SUMMERCOMBE WOOD THREATENED BY PROGRESS.

19. The Sacrifice

Swiftly, Polly ran her eyes down the column of print. "If a proposal by the County Council meets with approval from the Department of the Environment, the village of Switchwick will win a long-awaited reprieve. A new by-pass is being planned which will divert traffic wishing to gain access to the motorway from the existing road, which passes through the village.

"For some time now residents have complained that the ever-increasing volume of traffic has brought dust, noise, and atmospheric pollution to the village, and lately fears have been expressed that there could be danger to life and property. Residents of Summercombe, too, will welcome the news. They claim that the junction of their road with the

Switchwick road is hazardous, and that there has already been one near fatal accident there.

"The proposed route will carry the by-pass along the side of the hill, below the iron age fort, and across land which is mostly unproductive and infertile. The main casualty will be Summercombe wood, which will be divided in half by the new road."

There was a large-scale map of the area, with a dotted line drawn to indicate the path of the proposed new road. It was smudged and indistinct, but Polly could see that Summercombe wood was in danger of being bisected along its whole length, and worse, the by-pass would skirt the front of her garden. She stood looking at the map for a few moments, knowing that Mrs. Fletcher was eagerly waiting to see her reaction. She took a deep breath, determined at least that she would not give the woman the satisfaction of seeing that she was distressed.

So she was smiling as she turned to face Mrs. Fletcher. "I'm afraid the *Advertiser* is a little premature with its news. After all, this is, as yet, only a proposal, little more than a pipe dream. It's hardly fair, in my view, to raise people's hopes when so much still needs to be considered."

Mrs. Fletcher was nettled. "Everyone I've spoken to so far thinks it's a fine idea. I've no doubt myself that it will go through as planned. After all, the council exists to serve the rate payers, and if they want the new road, the council must surely build it."

"I hope the rate payers can afford it," mused Polly. "My yearly contribution won't go far, I know."

"The country's rich enough," sniffed Mrs. Fletcher. "And anyhow, they'll probably get a grant from the Department of the Environment, since the new road is to serve the motorway." She omitted to mention that if the new road was built across Summercombe wood and the adjoining fields along the shoulder of the hill, Mr. Fletcher would be handsomely reimbursed for land which had become nothing more than a nuisance to him.

Polly took her milk and fled, but in spite of her apparent lack of concern, her heart was heavy as she made her way back to the cottage. As she turned in at the gate she tried to visualize a major road snaking across the fields. Already in her imagination she could hear the sullen roar of diesel engines, an unending procession of heavy trucks thundering past by day and by night. As she stood meditating a blackbird flew to the hedge with a worm in his bill. For a few moments he perched on a dead branch, and as Polly watched she heard him warble a snatch of song.

She wondered how many people knew that a blackbird could sing with a beakful of worms. How many cared? How many ever got a chance to find out? How many could afford the luxury of standing in the fragrance and peace of an evening in spring, and hear the song of a bird? Suddenly she was aware of the privilege of her position, in enjoying the best of both worlds. She accepted without question the gifts of progress. She took for granted a pure water supply, skilled medical service, and an efficient police force. She had electric light, television, her record player, and more clothes than she could ever wear out, a greater store of material possessions than perhaps any previous resident of the cottage ever had. Without these objects, and other benefits, would she still retain the numinous sense of wonder and awe for the rest of the natural world, or would she become just another drudge, ill nourished and in poor health, cursing an alien environment?

She did not know, but she was honest enough with herself to admit that perhaps she did not care to find out. She also had to admit that if she herself expected and took for granted a high standard of living, then she had no right to deny it to anyone else. The new by-pass was intended as part of that system by which living standards were maintained, for the motorways brought petrol for her car to her garage, petrol derived from oil that lay fathoms deep beneath the North Sea. The motorway carried new potatoes from the coasts of Cornwall and Wales to the cities, and fertilizers from the manufacturers to the fields. They brought everything from sugar to cigarettes, from new books to nylon underwear to the local shops, and if the system was not ideal, at least it worked. One day there might be a better transport system, for after all the railways had replaced the canals, and in a very short space of time the motorways had ousted the railways. Meanwhile, mankind had to learn to live with the motorway.

Polly found herself reflecting rather bitterly that this was a society that would not dream of depriving her of her material possessions, without being given extremely good cause, but which would, without any misgivings, rob her of the immeasurable and indefinable wealth of her surroundings, and so considerably reduce the quality of her life. Immediately, she realized that this was perhaps unfair of her. The building of the by-pass would greatly improve the quality of life for the residents of Switchwick, and when it was built perhaps they would be able to stand in their gardens and hear a blackbird sing. If they wanted to, that was.

Polly suspected that the majority would be more concerned about the quality of reception on their television sets. Certainly the planners were motivated by the economics of speedy transport, rather than the welfare of the villagers, and anyway, the residents were not gaining anything new, but merely getting back the peace and quiet they once enjoyed. This was not progress; it was maintaining the status quo.

She herself was the sacrifice, and not much of one at that. She was well past middle age, and she had no dependents. She might well be dead before the by-pass opened, or unfit to manage alone. Already she could feel twinges of rheumatism in her shoulders and hips after a day in the garden.

Suddenly she pulled herself together, scolding herself for what in anyone else she would have regarded as maudlin self-pity. She marched into the house, put the milk in the refrigerator, and poured herself a large iced tea. "Here's to progress," she said aloud, and then corrected herself. "No, to Mother Nature. She always wins, in the end."

Of one thing she was certain. She could not appeal against the planning of the new road. It meant too much to everyone else. To fight a lone battle would merely succeed in making her very unpopular, and it would be a long and wearisome struggle that would in the end prove futile. She would just have to wait and watch events, and if those events made life too unbearable, she could always sell out and move somewhere else. After all, no dream lasted forever.

Suddenly she remembered the badgers and the wood, and realized that she was not the only sacrifice to progress. The badgers, too, would be dispossessed of their home, as would all living things that lay in the path of the proposed by-pass. Did it matter? Life had survived the ice ages of the past. Surely it could survive this ice age, when glaciers of concrete crept across the island, and vast areas of the naked earth lay buried not under snow fields, but under tons of bricks and mortar.

Was it possible that a breed of man would one day emerge who could learn to live as one with the rest of the natural world? There had been such people in the past, and she wished fervently that once again it could be so. Then she thought of herself and her garden. She flattered herself that it was semi-natural, and used no pesticides or herbicides, nor any artificial fertilizers. She liked to think it was a haven for wildlife, especially birds, but in the vegetable plot no weeds were permitted. Each week she ruthlessly destroyed thousands of small plants she would not dream of harming in woodland or hedgerow, and she waged continual war against slugs and snails, caterpillars and greenfly, ants' nests and earwigs. It was no good denying it, she was as guilty as the next person in waging war on the wild, and the by-pass, when it came, would be no more than a logical extension of her activities in the garden. As long as mankind needed to eat, the war would continue.

She was still brooding as she set off through the woods to take up her vigil on the ash stump. The blackthorn had shed its bloom, and the white petals lay like snowdrifts among the purple haze of the hyacinths. Rooks were calling to each other as they drifted lazily overhead, and a thrush sang in a rich contralto. The aroma of the woods rose strong and sensual on the warm evening air, a scent so pungent that it was almost animal, and everywhere the beauty of the new green leaf was bewildering in its rippling diversity of shade and texture, like the silks and satins of an empress's wardrobe, spilled out for all to admire. Some half-forgotten lines of poetry came to her mind, lines written by Patrick Pearse, the Irish rebel leader, on the eve of his execution for his part in the Easter Rising, 1916:

> "The beauty of this world has made me sad,
> This beauty that will pass."

She had to permit herself a wry smile at the recollection of the next lines.

> "Sometimes my heart has shaken with great joy,
> To see a leaping squirrel on a tree."

Thomas had "shaken with great joy," and his joy had quickly turned to anguish.

She reached the ash stump and climbed into it, settling herself comfortably on the cushion she had brought with her. Below her the clearing lay silent and empty, as the green-dappled light of day slowly turned to yellow in the setting sun. There was no breeze, and as Polly sat watching and listening, her senses slowly became attuned to the tiny sounds that dropped into the pool of silence, the buzz of a beetle, the soft clap of a bird's wings, a slow, smooth rustle that marked the passage of a snake. Stealthily, secretly, the magic of the woodlands wooed and possessed her, so that she became as one with the ancient oaks and the fragrant fertile earth, and the affairs of mankind grew small and far away.

Suddenly, a loud sniffing noise alerted her and brought her back to reality. Peering down into the clearing, she saw to her delight that a badger had emerged from one of the openings and was standing in the arena, its back to her and its head nodding as it stared into the trees. As she watched, it flopped over onto one haunch and proceeded to scratch its flank vigorously. Then it rolled over and repeated the process on the other flank, its claws making a loud rasping noise against its hide.

Polly was surprised to find that her mouth was dry and her heart was beating furiously. She was terrified that she would cough or sneeze, or make some movement that would alert the animal to her presence. She held her breath, as Borun lurched to his feet, gave himself a thorough shaking, and padded leisurely away to the latrine area. A few minutes later he returned to the mouth of the set, and to Polly's joy a second badger emerged, to repeat the process of shaking and scratching.

For a short while the pair pottered about the clearing, scraping at the ground here and there, and poking around at the entrances to the sets. Polly did not realize it, but the two badgers had picked up the scent of Thomas after his visit on the previous day, and were now checking to see if they had received a further visitation. Fortunately, Polly had not gone near the sets, and the badgers, finding only stale, cold scent, were unperturbed.

Without warning, Borun moved off into the wood, and Handa, after watching him depart, returned to the darkness of the set and her cubs. The clearing, which a moment before had seemed alive with small and busy people, once more lay silent and deserted, and Polly was aware of a sense of deflation and loss. For the very first time since she had moved into her cottage, she felt lonely.

She was also stiff and cramped and cold, and she had forgotten to bring a torch with her. The sun had dipped below the shoulder of the hill, and already the fields below the wood were bathed in purple mist. If she was to find her way home through the wood in safety, she would have to be on her way. Quietly, she slipped out of the ash stump and stole away.

20. Woodland Encounter

The following night she returned to the wood, and her vantage point in the ash stump, and once again she was rewarded with a glimpse of Borun and Handa. It was the same on the next night, and the next, and gradually the nocturnal visits grew to be an obsession with her. Throughout the day she followed her normal routine, without giving more than a passing thought to what she had come to refer to as the little gray bears of the wood. But each evening, as the sun began to slant toward the shoulder of the hill, and the shadows of the woodland lengthened beneath the trees, the confines of the cottage became almost unbearable to her, and she felt drawn to the twisting path beneath the oaks.

Sometimes she was rewarded with a glimpse of the adult

badgers. At other times they failed to appear. It did not matter. It was the ageless brooding mystery of the twilight that drew her, quickening her senses, sharpening her hearing, enhancing her sense of smell, as darkness deepened and her eyesight became of secondary importance. Each evening she returned to the cottage, stiff, cold, and itching from mosquito bites, barking her shins as she stumbled through the wood.

Not surprisingly perhaps, at the end of a week she succumbed to a feverish chill, which confined her at first to bed, and then to the cottage. Gradually she grew stronger, and as health returned, so did the urge to visit the woods. At the end of a fortnight she could bear it no longer. The day had been warm and sunny, with the promise of a mild night, and she felt fit and strong again. Dressed in warm clothes, and carrying her cushion, she set off.

She was surprised to see how far spring had advanced since her last outing. Entering the woods was like plunging into a deep green pool, a dim-lit lake where all was liquid movement. Late-foraging bumblebees droned heavily among the thick clusters of blossom, that clung like clotted cream to the spiky twigs of the hawthorns, and all around the air was loud with bird song, as from every thicket and brake each individual songster proclaimed his territorial rights for others of his kind to heed.

She settled into the ash stump, a little shaky and breathless, but eager to see what the night would bring. A half-hour passed, and gradually the bird song diminished in volume, until at last there was only the robin, still staking his claim from the top of a sycamore tree. The thin, high song ceased abruptly as the hoot of an owl echoed down through the trees, and in an interval of silence the dusk deepened in the valley.

Then Borun emerged, and a few seconds later the clearing was alive with bustle and noise, as the three cubs poured out of the set. Spellbound, Polly watched them begin a wild and joyous romp, racing in and out of the bushes, yelping and bickering and chasing each other's tails. For some twenty minutes the cubs played, lying in ambush and pouncing on each other, until the games ended in a prolonged and strenuous wrestling match, with all three rolling in the dust. Handa and Borun kept watch, making sure that no cub strayed too far, but otherwise interfering little with the cubs' boisterous play.

A vigorous grooming session followed. Handa inspected each protesting cub in turn, holding it down with a firm forepaw, and releasing it only when she was satisfied that the required standards of cleanliness had been met. It was late now, and the moon had risen, filling the arena with silver light, and plunging the bushes into deep shadow. Suddenly, Polly realized that she was alone. The badgers had faded into the night. She waited a while, half hoping they would return, but also giving them time to get well clear, so that she would not alarm them as she made her way back to the cottage. She could hardly wait for twilight to come again.

The long day passed, a day of increasing concern for Polly. She had slept badly, her dreams disturbed by woodland scenes, through which small, gnomelike creatures capered madly in the moonlight. She woke in the early hours, wondering what was to be the fate of the badgers, and then could not sleep again. Would the sets be destroyed by the building of the by-pass? Would the youngsters have left home by then? She did not know. She would have to get maps, and try to relate the proposed route to the position of the sets. Even then she could not be sure, for the line of the by-pass was not yet fixed. She would just have to wait until she had more positive information to go on. She tried to dismiss the problem from her mind, but it kept returning, in spite of all she could do to keep herself occupied.

She was relieved when at last the day was far enough advanced to allow her to escape to the woods. There at least she would find solace, and relief from her anxieties. The evening was sultry and humid, and in the distance the mutter of thunder heralded the coming of a storm. Nevertheless, she set off, her cushion under her arm, moving slowly through the trees.

Long practice had taught her to move without sound, so that now she could pick her way through the woods without rustling a leaf or stirring a branch. Thus she had come to learn much more about the ways of the woodland, and was rewarded by small cameos; a stoat poised in a clearing, one paw raised as its nose quested the air, a hen pheasant nervously leading her chicks across a path, a grass snake lying coiled beneath the fern. All these images she stored lovingly in her memory. She was alert to sounds too, and could distinguish between the short, sharp rustle that told of a bank vole diving for its nest, and the scratching of a lizard as it scurried for cover over the dried leaves, a sound exactly like a pen nib scratching over parchment.

So when she heard a rustle in the undergrowth, a few yards away to her right, she stopped and listened. It came again, and at first she thought that it was just a blackbird scratching in the leaves, a sound that had often deceived her in the past, but then she heard what sounded to her like an exasperated groan. She moved forward cautiously, not knowing quite what manner of beast might be hinding in the woods, but curious to find out.

A bearded face stared out from a clump of elder, a face with gimlet dark eyes and black curly hair. For one idiotic moment she thought she had come face to face with the woodland god Pan, but just as she was beginning to doubt her sanity a twig snapped under her foot, and the face spoke. "Is anyone there?"

Pulling herself together, and trying to keep her voice under control, Polly answered, "What is it?"

"I wonder if you would care to render a little assistance here."

Striving not to laugh, so great was her relief, Polly climbed up the slope. The voice was so precise and controlled, the request so polite, that in this setting it sounded incongruous.

It was not Pan who lay half reclining in the thicket, but a man, well past middle age, attired in a neat jacket of Norfolk green, with a matching shirt and tie. He made no attempt to rise as she approached, but contented himself with a rather deprecatory wave of his hand. "I'm afraid I've got myself into a rather ridiculous predicament here. Your arrival is most timely, ma'am."

"What happened?" queried Polly.

The man pointed in the direction of his foot. "I slipped, walking along the side of the hill, and my foot has somehow got trapped under a root."

Polly looked, and sure enough the man's leg was gripped tight, just above the ankle, between a tough elder root and a rock. "Perhaps, if I could get your boot off . . ." she began.

"I fancy my foot is now too swollen, but if you could loosen the laces, it might be more comfortable."

He sighed in relief as Polly did as he asked, but it was clear to her that she could not remove the boot without cutting it. She had no way of knowing whether the ankle was broken or merely sprained, and she hesitated to touch it in case she caused further injury. Suddenly it occurred to her that the obvious solution was to cut through the root.

"If you could just be patient for a little while longer," she said. "My cottage is not far away. I'll go back and get a saw, and then you'll soon be free."

"I would be most grateful," said the man. "I promise you I won't go anywhere."

Polly laughed. Then she remembered her cushion. "Perhaps if you put this behind your head," she offered. "It might be more comfortable."

"Such luxury," sighed the man, settling back. "I'm so

glad you came along. If I might make one more small request? My haversack is lying just up the hill where I dropped it. In it are my cigarettes and matches. With them I can wait content."

Polly scrambled further up the hill and retrieved the haversack from the fern. It was surprisingly heavy, as though it was full of rocks, and the handle of a hammer stuck out of the flap, but it was not until she was halfway back to the cottage that its significance struck her. Even then there was no time for speculation, for the impending storm was now much nearer. The skies were darkening, and an ominous breeze ruffled the leaves of the trees.

Still, she voiced her question in the form of a comment, as she sawed through the elder root with a small bow saw. "You're a geologist, Mr. . . ."

"Firth, ma'am, Rupert Firth. Yes, I am. That is why I find myself here, and all because a group of megalomaniac bureaucrats think they can build a by-pass here."

Polly's interest quickened, but just then the root parted, and the geologist was free. Gingerly he stood up, testing his leg with his weight. "Not broken, I think," he grunted. "Only sprained, and swollen with the constriction."

"I brought a long-handled broom back with me," said Polly. "I'm afraid I'm not strong enough to bear your weight, but if you put the head of the broom under your armpit, you can use it as a crutch."

"A splendid idea," murmured Firth. "I must be in favor with the god Pan for him to have sent you, of all people, to save me."

"I thought you were he," laughed Polly "when I first saw you."

"Oh, he was very near," said Firth seriously. "I felt his presence just before you arrived. Not for nothing did he give his name to panic. Fortunately, he's a jokey sort of fellow. He likes to tease."

Polly shivered. "You've probably noticed that there is a storm brewing. I think we ought to vacate the woods as quickly as you are able. We'll make for my cottage, and then I can look at that ankle."

A flash of lightning gave point to her remark, and they set off through the woods, he leaning on his makeshift crutch, and she following, burdened with cushion, saw, and haversack.

21. The Geology Lesson

Twenty minutes later Rupert Firth sat in Polly's armchair, sipping some hot tea as Polly applied cold compresses to his ankle, while outside the full fury of the storm unleashed itself upon the woods. Rupert glanced out the window and shuddered, thinking about his predicament had he not been rescued. "Miss Shaw," he began, "you really are a paragon. I can't think how I can ever repay you for your resourcefulness and kindness."

Polly could, but for the moment she held her peace.

"My chances of rescue seemed so slim," continued Firth. "And then you came along. It's none of my business, I know, but could you satisfy my vulgar curiosity by telling me why a lady of your mature years was walking through the woods at that hour, carrying, of all things, a cushion?''

"Simple," said Polly. "I was setting out to watch badgers.''

"Ah yes," nodded Firth, as though it was the most natural thing in the world for an elderly lady to do. "I saw the sets earlier today. The whole hillside is honeycombed with them.''

"They won't be there much longer if the by-pass is built," said Polly quietly.

There was a long silence, as Firth sipped his tea. Finally, he spoke. "I expect that while I was trapped under that root I was delirious and babbling, so that if in one of my more lucid moments I let slip certain information, I could trust you to treat it with the same confidence that a nurse or a doctor would?"

Polly grinned. The more she saw of this man the more she liked him. "Yes, you can trust me. I gather your report won't be a good one.''

Firth's eyebrows shot up. "My reports are always good. Models of accuracy and detail. Whether they are favorable or not to the parties concerned is of no consequence to me. I am a consultant geologist, and I get the same fee whatever my findings. My opinion, which I believe is quite well respected in several countries, is bound in the end to be upheld. What do you know about geology?"

"Nothing," admitted Polly.

"You ought to know something," said Firth sternly. "You can't begin to understand the hills and valleys unless you know something about their anatomy. Have you a few slices of bread?"

Polly got to her feet. "I'm so sorry. I quite forgot. You must be starving.''

Firth laughed. "Please. I want the bread for quite a different purpose. Fetch it, and you'll see.''

Polly brought four slices of bread on a plate, and Firth stacked them neatly, one on top of the other. ''The rocks that form the backbone of this hill may be anything up to two hundred million years old,'' he began. ''They are sedimentary rocks. That is to say, they are formed of sand washed down by rivers long extinct, or blown by winds from ancient deserts. These rocks once lay on the floor of a shallow sea, shifting sands, moved here and there by the currents until they were coated with a calcareous solution, and then compressed by further layers of sediment until they became limestone.

''From time to time the sea dried, and boulder clay covered the limestone. Then came a layer of sand, and then the seas returned, to lay down a layer of limestone again. So these layers were built up, like these slices of bread, with perhaps a smear of butter or jam in between. The first thing to remember, then, is that sedimentary rocks are always laid down on top of each other, almost horizontally, and then compressed, so that after a few thousand years the layer is about a foot thick. The second thing to bear in mind is that the oldest rocks are at the bottom.''

A peal of thunder drowned his voice, and he glanced up at Polly. ''Am I boring you?'' he asked.

Polly shook her head, and he continued. ''The fury of the elements tonight is nothing compared with the storms that have raged in ages past, that swept the sediments down to the sea. Now the earth lies in chains, and we tend to think she is overpowered, but from time to time she stirs, she moves, and strives to break her bonds.''

He took the slices of bread by the four corners, bending the sides upward, so that all four sloped inward and down toward the center. ''Sometimes this happens, and we call it a syncline, but sometimes this formation occurs.''

He pressed the corners of the bread to the plate and pushed inward, so that the center of the top slice rose in a hump, forced upward by the other slices underneath. ''We call this an anticline, and as you can see, the layers of rock that form the hill slope down and out, so that if one was to cut into the side, or otherwise disturb the formation, the slabs would slide away downhill.''

"And this hill is an anticline?'' queried Polly.

"Right,'' said Firth. "And if anyone was to interfere with it, then, on such a night as this, as water seeped between the layers of rock, lubricating their surfaces, parts of the hill could well slide away. In fact, I would go so far as to say that they definitely would slide, only I couldn't predict quite when or where.''

"Could the hillside not be buttressed, to keep it from sliding?'' asked Polly.

Firth nodded. "Sure. But in this instance it would have to be supported above and below the road, and whoever undertook the roadwork would have to be prepared to write a blank check, for no accurate estimate of the cost could be made. Even then the work could not be guaranteed.''

Polly felt a great surge of relief. "So the by-pass will never be built?''

"It will be built somewhere, no doubt. Probably along the floor on the opposite side of the valley. You'll see it from here, but it will be at least a mile away at its nearest point. Oh, my report will be rejected, and my clients will employ commercial geologists, who will take the taxpayers' money for giving the sort of answers the planners want to hear to their questions. There may be trial borings, but in the end they will have to give in. If a major trunk road was being planned, or a motorway, things might be different, but for a few miles of village by-pass, no politician is going to risk his career by squandering public funds.''

Suddenly Polly felt ten years younger. "Well, Mr. Firth, you've amply repaid me for rescuing you. For a moment, when I first realized why you were in the wood, I was tempted to leave you where you were.''

"Call me Rupert,'' begged Firth. "I think that is about the

one thing you wouldn't be capable of. And now, somehow, I must relieve you of the burden of my presence."

"On a night like this? You'll do no such thing. I'll fix a meal, and then you can occupy the spare bed. I'm sure that at our age we can dispense with the proprieties. In the morning I'll drive you to the doctor to get that leg examined."

A sudden thought struck her, one that filled her with unaccountable dismay. "Oh, I didn't think. Someone might be wondering where you were . . . might be concerned."

Firth shook his head. "There's no one. I'm a widower, have been for a long time. I had planned to find a hotel for the night."

"That's settled then," said Polly. "Help yourself to more tea while I scramble some eggs."

She was abashed to discover she was blushing, and scurried away into the kitchen, where she rattled plates while she scolded herself for being a stupid old maid. All the same, she could not suppress a lilting happiness at the thought that whatever else this night's work had begun, it had laid the foundations of what she hoped would be a long friendship.

Much later, Firth raised his cup to the storm. "To you, Pan," he murmured. "Thanks, you noisy bounder."

Polly smiled, remembering an earlier defiant toast she had made. "No," she corrected. "To Mother Nature. She always wins, in the end."

Epilogue

Work began in earnest on the new by-pass late one December. At the end of the first day, as the excavators ground to a standstill, and the mechanics slouched wearily over the wasteland they had created, back to their waiting cars, a badger stood in a thorn thicket, his striped head nodding slightly as he surveyed the scene. Borun and his kind would not alter their ways, and it may be that in their very resistance to change they have sealed their own fate. Yet equally it could be argued that by continually changing his lifestyle, man might one day hit upon one which, all unforeseen, could prove to be the one that would ensure his own extinction. Perhaps, indeed, he has already chosen that path.

Further down the valley Polly, too, gazed across the fields

at the raw yellow scar, now mercifully becoming veiled in the gauze of the twilight. If, as she fervently believed, all nature was part of a whole, and the universe revolved with meaning, and if man was part of nature, as she was sure he was, then even the inscrutable working of his mind was part of the plan, however aberrant and devious his behavior might appear to be.

Certainly it was unbelievable that an intellect that could conceive an oak tree in an acorn would permit a mere man to wreck the plan. In spite of this, she knew she could not complacently accept the world as it was, as long as she lived, and carried within her the realization of what it could be. Perhaps this knowledge, too, was part of the plan, and it might be that the very possession of life prevented her from learning its secret. Death might provide the key, and with this thought she was content, accepting without rancor the knowledge that she had but a relatively short time to wait.

At the edge of the thorn thicket Borun glanced skyward, and a star shone in his eye, the same star that had shone on the unseeing eye of his dead father, that had shone on the building of Stonehenge. How many more changes might the star yet witness, before the sun burnt itself out, leaving the world locked in a pall of ice? For the badgers of Summercombe, and Western civilization, time was perhaps running out. The badgers at least had for the moment won a short reprieve.